Death's Midwives

Ontario Review Press Translation Series
General Editor, Leif Sjoberg

Death's Midwives

Stories by
Margareta Ekström

Translated from the Swedish by
Eva Claeson

With a Preface by
Nadine Gordimer

Ontario Review Press/Princeton

English-language translation copyright © 1985 by Eva Claeson.
Preface copyright © 1985 by Nadine Gordimer.
Most of these stories were originally published in Swedish:
in *Överfallet* (1963), *Husliga scener* (1964), *Födelseboken* (1967),
Förhållandet till främmande makter (1972), *Människodjuren* (1974),
Dödens barnmorskor (1975), and *Kärlekens utland* (1982), all
copyright © by Margareta Ekström.
All rights reserved.
Printed in the U.S.A.
"When We Are Home Alone We Dance All Around the House,"
"Death's Midwives," and "The Night Between the Second and the Third"
first appeared in English in *The Ontario Review*;
"Hebe Laughs" in *Vogue*.

Library of Congress Cataloging in Publication Data

Ekström, Margareta, 1930–
Death's midwives.

(Ontario Review Press translation series)
1. Ekström, Margareta, 1930– — Translations,
English. I. Title.
PT9876.15.K77A23   1985   839.7'374   85-18774
ISBN 0-86538-046-5
ISBN 0-86538-047-3 (pbk.)

Distributed by PERSEA BOOKS, Inc.
225 Lafayette St., New York, NY 10012

Contents

Preface by Nadine Gordimer   vii

When We Are Home Alone We Dance All Around the House   1

Perfect   14

The King Is Threatened   26

Balzac's Valet   44

Hebe Laughs   56

Death's Midwives   69

The Child's Garden   84

Left Alone   106

The Nothingness Forest   115

The Eagle Cage   124

The Night Between the Second and the Third   135

Preface

In Sweden, translations go almost all one way: from other languages into Swedish. I myself have among Swedish writers close friends of whose work I have been able to read one tantalizing book, or none. Much as I enjoy the particular qualities of mind available through personal relationships, these have been an ironic reversal of my conviction that it is knowing the work that counts, not hobnobbing with the writer.

A few of Margareta Ekström's stories have appeared in English translation in literary magazines; just enough to make one turn with expectation and curiosity to this collection of her stories at last made available in English. Expectation because of the sharp-edged delicacy, humor and fresh, intelligent emotion brought to apparently homely themes in the few stories already known, and curiosity, yes—because Swedish society, with its social justice and individual freedoms already achieved, produces something between awe and jealous criticism in almost the whole of the rest of the Western World, which either despairs of attaining such goals or, if it has reached them in some measure, of holding them.

Swedes are exotic. To us in the violent and confused states of aspiration, among the glass banking temples mirroring the homeless, the broken, the discarded aged in the streets, the safari tourists overflying the starving in the bush, the car bombs, tear gas, and assassinations in the cities, the lives of Swedish people are sometimes unimaginable; a higher state, if one has the honesty not snobbishly to romanticize suffering as "real life" and to remind oneself that the object of social justice is to banish the necessity for suffering. What are they like, those who are free from want, and the spectacle of want? Crushed countless times, like the body of a cat on a highway, the broken memory is picked up. There *is* something called the pursuit of happiness. That was supposed to be what struggle was all about.

Margareta Ekström's stories take place in the state of the pursuit of happiness. Let no-one confuse this with Nirvana, or disdain it as trivial. To be free of those needs whose satisfaction society controls—states of hunger, injustice, spiritual and mental oppression—is to be free to meet with full attention and dignity a life contained by the inexorable structure of birth and death.

Yet Ekström is not concerned with an after- or before-life, with any speculations of immortality. Life is a given: it is not conceived as something to be earned, or to be extended beyond the body in which it is incarnate. The people in her stories are living in the heightened state of total awareness of being through which *she* strives to create. That is her gift. They are *informed* by the forces the writer herself feels, and she is beautifully able to convey; the twig jumps in her hands and she unerringly directs the reader: there life runs. Ekström's theme is most often the physical limits of existence itself. The meaning of birth and death she finds in the flesh: its feel, its smell, its sexual transformations. Therefore it is natural that children and old people should be her principal subjects. She writes of both with a tenderness whose honest sensuality precludes sentimentality. To appropriate her own words, she moves on that "razor-fine edge between buzz and silence, struggle and immobility." When the buzz of the tiniest insect stops, as when an old dying woman thinks she is speaking but there is no voice left for the nurse to hear, the body has come to a stop. The possibilities of the human story have come to a stop. But what richness to capture in between! The finest story in the collection, "Death's Midwives," moves on the plane of experience outside time, joining dying and giving birth as aspects of a woman's concentration "on what is happening inside her body." The moment at which the story ends is her death, yet it also seems the moment at which she is giving birth: a perfect circle, enclosing both a life whose meaning lies not in chronology, historical time, and a writer's stylistic victory over the determinants staked out as beginning and end.

Loneliness and communion are what this writer understands as providing the real tension of polarity within the circle. Here her territory is not exotic Sweden but what we all have to construct somehow on even the shakiest ground, "the common home, the little house human beings helped each other to create to protect them from the icy winds of the inexplicable and the black holes of meaninglessness."

Literature is part of that little house of mutual pleasures and bonds, that common home. Margareta Ekström helps to furnish it for us with images that are a pleasure to more senses than that of the reading eye. Some bring the special cool pungency of frail Northern nature outside the window, and others add to the specificity of place, and of the humble objects that make it so, an aphoristic twist: "The variously colored ends of the different seasons are tied together like rags in rugs."

It is true that one sees things differently when one is free to engage in the pursuit of happiness. It is also true that from there, given the skill of this writer, one can show people things that they have looked at but never seen before. And in the intriguing story "The Night Between the Second and the Third," Margareta Ekström also makes it clear that frightening moral choices are never absent, anywhere, between birth and death.

—Nadine Gordimer

When We Are Home Alone We Dance All Around the House

G. LEAVES FIRST. Big G. in his light-brown overcoat and with his woolen scarf wrapped once around his neck. He whistles and it echoes in the marble staircase.
Then little U., his wife, leaves. She stops short in the hall, has forgotten something. She picks up the telephone receiver and puts it down again. She runs into the kitchen and grabs the grocery list that big G. had promised to take. She shouts into the children's room: "Don't forget the dog, and dress warmly because it's cold outside, and see you at dinner, my darlings!"
One day, when U. called from downstairs, both Viveka and Matthew were sitting in the dinette with their hot chocolate, and they didn't say a word. "Funny kids," U. mumbles as she fiddles with the lock. The door closes behind her with a click. Clickety-clack, her heels go down the stairs, then the outer door sucks shut and you can hear her car start.

I'm still in bed. I stretch and then I pass my hand over my cheeks: the stubble makes a rasping sound, as when you touch silk with rough hands. I rub my forehead vigorously. The skin moves back and forth with my hand a bit and then stops. I imagine little root filaments that grow into flesh and bone. They keep the skin from sliding off like a glove. I scratch my neck and my back as far down as I can reach. I roll over onto my left side and smile into the pillow. I've borrowed G.'s pajamas. They're a little too big. I check how much. I often have an erection in the morning, and then they fit perfectly.

I reach the window with my left hand and push it up. This is their spring. It is very cold, but nice. The air feels brisk against my face and my palate—I try to swallow some. Their very insignificant spring flowers gleam weakly from their beds. The birds sound like mechanical toys. People talk a lot about them, they know the different sorts, their names and habits. They talk as though they were still living in some sort of primitive era in which they have to know all about the edibility of plants and the egg-laying periods of birds. But they don't pick or collect any of these—only talk about them, just the way my friends in France talk about opera stars and politicians.

At that point she is already standing in the doorway looking at me. I know this because I can feel the draft on my neck. I laugh and creep back under the covers. Sometimes she goes away and gets the breakfast tray ready. Sometimes she assaults me like a fury, pinches me and fights, pulls the pillow out from under my head and throws it on the floor. But the room is so small that it lands on the bookshelf and scatters the dust from big G.'s books.

I lie down on my back and pull up my knees so that my legs form a slide. She is a little too big for it. But as soon as Matthew is gone you can amuse her like a little child. Sometimes he leaves late and stands in the doorway, the day's first cigarette in his mouth, and smiles sadly. He feels left out. He is fourteen and Viveka is eleven. I like him just as much as I like Viveka. But he feels more aloof, isn't as open as she is, doesn't play like she does. There is a special game that Viveka and I play. He, Matthew, can never be part of it. Even though he can—when he is, just as now, standing there leaning against the doorway, listening to our babbling with somewhat of a bitter smile and with the acrid and cheap cigarette smoke rising to his eyes and making them water—after all, it's so early in the morning... yes, even though he can then feel a thrill of desire to creep into my bed and to forget all the old rules. I know. I felt it myself. Then he takes his schoolbag which is always packed with care, and walks down the steps. Sometimes he whistles, just like big G.

Then we are completely alone in the house.

We have our coffee sitting on the sofa in the living room. I put on some pants, so as not to feel so naked—once she smiled just like Matthew when she saw how awkwardly eager I was to get dressed for her sake. But I keep on my pajama top. She likes it because it has red and black stripes. She calls me her toreador. I laugh so much I have to double over. I did see a bullfight once, at home when I was seventeen, and I fainted. I have sat on four different committees for the abolition of bullfighting, and I tell her so. She blows imaginary cigarette smoke out of her nose, snorts, dances around in a circle and says: "I can call you whatever I want to."

And she does: Kangaroo, Little One, Husband,

Baby, Elephant, Porcupine. Sometimes Juan. Which doesn't sound at all like the Juan that is my name. More like a soft cat sound. My name Swedified to a "yan."

We sit close to each other on the expensive Dux sofa. She puts her hand on my knee possessively. I recognize a little of U. in her—same pride in her face but with a funny disappointed pout behind it, like when she looks at G. in the evening.

I have so much fun. I have a hard time leaving the house. Finally I manage to get dressed, although Viveka tries to keep me from it sometimes. I tie my tie, she unties it. I button the four buttons of my jacket, she unbuttons them. Lastly, with an affected wifely expression, she administers a goodbye kiss. I try to make it as light as I can, but she usually holds my face tightly and presses her wet little mouth against mine. I have to use force to free myself and then I hold her at arm's length. I have to be careful not to laugh at her then. Once I did and she hit me in the face as hard as she could. There is a word for girls like that in the country I come from. I heard it for the first time from the boys in the village. It wasn't used at the University—they had another word for it. They called girls who gave themselves "prostitutes." But the name for very young girls who were precocious had a beautiful, springlike sound. It reminded one of the dialect word for "morning bird"—or was it "morning glow"?

No, I mustn't laugh at her then. I must look her deep in the eyes "until it tickles in my stomach," she says. It isn't difficult to obey her. Then, when we have stood like that for a while, we must sigh longingly. Thereupon she usually whimpers dramatically in English: "Not yet, not yet!" like Greta Garbo in *The Twins*. And I make a wistful gesture of farewell, I throw her a kiss which is supposed to float through the air and land on her forehead. But sometimes I apparently exaggerate my role, because after closing the hall door behind me I hear her laugh, and while she peeks at my disappearing back through the mailbox slot the echo follows me down the stairs. Then I stand there on the bare empty square where the bus is supposed to come. The whole area looks like a science fiction movie. The quarry-like atmosphere of black stone and white concrete houses. The trees are newly planted in small rows, the way trees usually look on architects' drawings. I myself am a statistical figure: man waiting for a bus to the city. But the statistics lie: I don't belong to their society. Not even their political party. I am more of a strange bird than they can imagine. Their lack of curiosity is my greatest protection. There is so much money in this country that I almost go crazy. I can't even write about it to my brothers in the Organization and give them a true picture of this country's affluence. They would think I was lying despite their considerable knowledge about Swedish industrialism, the budget, balance of trade and taxation.

As I stand there waiting for my bus, I observe the sidewalk. It has a design in three shades of gray, and black and white besides. I tell myself that if we left out one shade of gray in this sidewalk, and let's say on the adjoining piazza as well, the money saved would be enough to build a school in my home village. It is a macabre joke, all of this. Sometimes I delight in being here, like being in a dream. Sometimes when it hits me that it is real, that it costs money, labor, I am disgusted. I feel like committing murder. My right hand moves to my left armpit to see if the excellent butcher knife that I got from Peta during the Civil War is still hanging in its leather strap under my left armpit. But my fingers only fumble over my perfectly tailored suit. The blazer has covered buttons. The pants have no cuffs. They're supposed to be that way this year. In this country.

In other words, I look good. Just like the sidewalk. If I left out the covered buttons... How much could I then send to the Organization?

I realize that I am touching my forehead and convulsing with laughter and saying "ay ay ay" at the same time, the way they do in my country. And just then the bus arrives and they all look at my black hair and strange gestures and think, "Damn foreigner," for that's what they think more often than they are willing to admit.

When I get off at Norra Bantorget, I only have a few blocks to walk to the office of my compatriots. They were able to rent it directly from the authorities. I think that's touching! We are not Social Democrats. Perhaps this country can afford that kind of generosity? But a nasty voice inside tells me that it is more likely because they are gullible and uninformed.

Pedro's secretary is a redhead. They are having an affair. That doesn't bother me, but I'm scared that the girl will decide to get pregnant and force him to leave the Organization for a better-paid job in this society. I feel my generosity straining the corners of my mouth. But I take them both out to lunch and we drink wine. The girl has been converted in this respect: Pedro has taught her to drink wine. What else has he taught her?

She spends all of her money on clothes. She thinks all foreigners are charming—discrimination just the same. She doesn't bother to vote, and reads only the inside pages of the newspaper. And with that pretty nothing Pedro risks having a child! Jesus Maria!

Afterwards I go to the newspaper stand at Central Station and buy all the foreign newspapers. I spend the afternoon at the Royal Library. I make telephone calls from the big soap bubbles of glass in the hallway. The students' high heels clatter as they pace back and forth while waiting for the telephone. I make a few calls that in a couple of weeks will mean death for Henri Vatista. They thumb through their little address books where the boyfriends' telephone numbers crowd in nervous rows. I don't grudge them their emancipation, quite the contrary. I only wish they used it more brazenly. My friend Ruth at the *Daily News* tells me about how girls used to dream of becoming the wives of professors or lieutenants. It is better now, she thinks. But I am afraid the difference is more that they dare take the initiative to become professors' and lieutenants' wives themselves, instead of only dreaming about it, but they don't dream of becoming professors or lieutenants themselves. Maybe I'm wrong. The suffragette type that I ran into on the committee turned out to be a flirt. The femme fatale at Berns nightclub was, when one got to know her, one of the most sensible people I have spoken with here in Stockholm. So what does one know? They are beautiful, that much I know. They are usually well-groomed and well-dressed. How much time it must take them!

I have dinner with an important man. Without ladies. My girlfriend the editor says that one day she will come and crash the party at my table at the restaurant, because she is so upset that I don't consider any ladies important enough to sacrifice a dinner to. But then I usually ask her to suggest some... "Well?" Then she says tentatively: "What about Marianne?" "Why should I meet with Marianne when actually it is always Sten who makes all the decisions and furthermore he has the more responsible position of the two?" "What about Dora? You would really benefit from getting to know Dora better." "But I have received a thousand times better information from the secretary of her department, because he has been in my country and we can speak my language." "That is just an unfortunate coincidence," my girlfriend says. But I say it is fortunate, because it always makes me happy to be able to speak my language with an intelligent human being. "You mean man," she says, and wants to argue. But I maintain that I mean "human being," and I also tell her that it is a pleasure to meet her, Ruth, any time, even when I have more important dinner guests. But actually, I would rather separate work from pleasure, and see her later in the evening.

One evening, at the Sturehof restaurant, I tell her about my day. About how it started with Viveka's little game, how it continued with the usual lunch with Pedro and the redhead. How I met the Minister of Finance, Hjalmar Mehr, and the Communist Party leader, Hermansson. Ruth is an intelligent woman. I very much enjoy acquainting her with my activities, up to a limit. There are things I don't even dare entrust to Pedro. Sometimes I think that my carefulness is beginning to turn into a persecution complex, but then something always happens in one of our daughter organizations that makes me feel too easygoing and I thank God that all is still going well. No, my secrecy is necessary until D-day. And then—then many people, and especially Ruth, won't want to know me any longer. And I, I'll manage perfectly well without them. Perfectly well. Or will I miss her? But missing someone is an unproductive state of being. An emotion for little children and for old people. I am neither young nor old enough to live with that emotion—it goes through me quickly, like an arrow without barbs. If I lean too long against a wall, I might get attached.

But Ruth only wants to hear more about Viveka. She brings up Nabokov's Lolita. And I laugh and say that I certainly don't let her sit on my lap. Not in that way. She looks dubious and suggests that I am most likely fooling myself. But I am not fooling myself. I know what I am doing, every minute. That's something we have to learn in the Organization. Or something we already knew before. For it is a special sort of person who is drawn to it, I've noticed that. And those who don't fit are quickly eliminated. By us, or by circumstances.

I catch the glance of an unknown lady. She is sitting at the table behind ours. Since Ruth often looks down into her plate while telling me something I am able to look at the unknown lady for a long time. I feel a purely animal desire for her. She has a wide mouth in the corners of which bread crumbs or bits of food get stuck continuously. She goes on talking with her companion without seeming to be aware that her mouth is so childishly messy. She moves her head eagerly like a bird. She wears a sleeveless dress of some dark, shiny fabric and a white shoulder strap falls constantly down over her arm and she makes a movement quick as lightning to poke it back under her dress. Every fifth or sixth time she turns her head, she catches my glance. When her companion goes to the telephone she stares at me openly. I am so serious that my temple bones feel as though they are cracking. But she has a mocking smile—I don't quite know whether she is making fun of me or of herself, or of the situation.

Ruth has wedged her foot between my legs as she usually does. I make believe that it is the unknown lady's foot, and it feels very pleasant. Ruth has suddenly begun to nag about this thing with Viveka. She is beginning to criticize me. Her face looks sour and older. I feel that I unreasonably like her less and less as we gradually and pleasurably, as usual, eat our way through the menu. I am sorry about feeling like this. But when the unknown lady leaves the restaurant without the slightest glance of farewell in my direction, I drop Ruth's foot and run after her.

Her companion isn't anywhere to be seen. She has stopped in the narrow passage between the two glass doors. Although a fat Swede is just trying to squeeze his equally fat wife into the restaurant, I take her elbow lightly and say: "Excuse me, but..." Then I begin to stammer like a schoolboy. And she looks at me, completely calm, with the same amused expression. Then she bends forward, gets up on her toes—she seems taller suddenly—and kisses me very tenderly on the cheek. I smile at her and get tears in my eyes. I'd like to know her name, address, meet her immediately, talk with her all night long... And before I've had time to think all of that she has gone through the door and disappeared.

On the way back to my table I run into her companion. We sway to the right and to the left in the ridiculous way you usually do when you pass someone in a narrow passage. Finally he takes hold of my shoulders with a big smile, and for a moment I think that he, as well, is about to kiss me, but he only holds me still in order to crowd by me, and then he half-lifts his hat when he disappears out into the street.

I give Ruth a plausible explanation—that I had suddenly recognized the lady, that she was an acquaintance from Paris, from the *Evening News*, from the Red Cross or from the moon. I become very calm and order our favorite liqueur with our coffee. I walk with her to her door and notice that she would very much like me to sleep with her.

Now, sitting on the bus and soon home at my artistically decorated sidewalk in the upper-class, sterile suburb which is considered only middle-class in this land of luxury, I try to arrive at some explanation for not having gone up with her. As soon as she had disappeared I began to like her again, very much. And with a sort of longing. Still, I'm glad I'll be home soon. Why did she become so sour, so quarrelsome? What had I said to hurt or worry her? Was it when I told her about Viveka and myself and said, "When we are home alone..."?

When I get off the bus there are stars as small as pinpricks dancing on the piazza pavement. The lights are out in Swedes' apartments, whose eyes are closed by Venetian blinds, white as hens' eyelids. I walk slowly across the square and raise my arms. Cold air slithers like lizards into my sleeves. I take a few dance-steps and hum. There is fun in the air. Something is awaiting me. Why is my mouth smiling? What is special about tomorrow?

In the elevator it occurs to me that Viveka doesn't sweat the way adolescent girls usually do. Like my own daughter. Last time I saw her she was fourteen. There was a heavy, fatty smell about her. But she is going to be a beauty. Viveka won't. She is skinny, almost bony. She has a faint spicy smell. Like those yellow buttons of flowers that grow at big G.'s country place. I'll ask him about them. Surely he'll know what they're called.

I have to laugh at Ruth. Lolita! Downright literary poisoning!

Inside the door, Viveka is standing waiting for me in her white batiste pajamas. She throws herself into my arms like a young fox. I carry her back and forth in the apartment and we both shush each other. Our laughter makes our stomachs jump, but we say "Shh! Quiet!" and look into each other's eyes. I don't know what to do with her. I can't find any place to put her down, to get rid of her. I just continue to carry her back and forth and she hangs like a rag doll in my arms. It is so quiet. You can hear the refrigerator motor start and a church bell rings far away in Vasa town.

When she first jumped into my arms she was as light as a feather boa, a little white fox-skin. Now she is so heavy and warm, so terribly warm. Perhaps she is ill? My arms will soon go numb. I wish Matthew would appear, grinning, in some dark corner. Anything at all —as long as there's an end to this. But everyone is asleep. She hangs motionlessly against my body and it is as though I have torn out my own heart and were walking around carrying it, for I cannot put her down for even a second.

I want to wake from that nightmare where I flee and flee from a house in flames, with enormous leaden shoes on my feet, and where I imagine I am saving a child. But it is instead one of the burning rafters that has fallen and that I, already dying, am carrying in my arms.

And when I meet her eyes tomorrow... I am already longing for the morning. When all is easy and cold, as is spring in this country, and full of laughter and tenderness, and we dance around wildly—all around the house.

Perfect

"Perfect," she thought. "Everything is perfect!"

The car was gliding soundlessly along the asphalt. They were swaying ahead on steel-blue plastic car cushions whose silver threads glistened softly in the light that came from shop windows. Soft radio music muffled the ticking of the taximeter.

She breathed in her own perfume and the reassuring smell of tweed, shaving lotion, man. She buried her face in her fur collar. "It really is delightful," she was thinking. "If Anja hadn't shown up this afternoon, I'd still be wearing that old perfume. It was all right too, or almost, that is. Just a little too sweet. That's what was wrong with it. A little bit too sweet. It wouldn't have felt this good. It would have felt like the tiniest little itch somewhere. The next best fragrance. But this, this is the best. Exactly my kind."

The car swerved around a corner, they were thrown against each other, then they sped on once more, along a straight stretch of road. At a red light she turned down the cuff of her glove and looked at her watch. It was O.K. They'd make it on time. Before, they always used to get to places at the last minute. A ridiculous habit. Sort of a childhood disease. Perhaps because you hadn't wanted to get up and go to school. As a result you had developed an aversion to all engagements, even nice ones. Like now for example: going to the theatre.

"I'm through behaving like a bohemian," she was thinking. "At least as far as engagements are concerned." And, as a matter of fact, they had gradually become much more punctual. Both of them. It was another step in the right direction. She hoped that there'd be many such steps.

While Nils was phoning for the taxi, she'd taken the flowers out of the pantry and put them on the table. They'd kept very well. He hadn't seen them when he'd passed through the room. She'd expected that. It was so easy to surprise him. Later, when they'd come home from the theatre, he'd probably stand in the doorway and say, "My goodness, look at that! You've already set the table! And flowers even...you just think of everything, don't you?"

He never thought about such little things. That made it even more fun for her. They were her own creations. She'd also taken out some candles. Colored candles for once. Actually, she felt that colored candles were cheap, in a way...sort of vulgar. But when she had discovered these, that were the same rust color as her stoneware dishes, she hadn't been able to resist. And then the flowers in the dark-blue glass jug. It was all just, yes, it all was really just perfect together.

She waited while he was paying for the taxi, and fingered her new glasses.

"No, I won't put them on before the lights go out,"

she decided. "I suppose that's ridiculous. Of course it's ridiculous. And vain. But...well, I'm not putting them on before the lights go out."

The checkroom wasn't crowded yet. They were so early, after all. When she turned around to look for the nearest mirror, she saw Nils' boss and his wife. It's a good thing I saw them even without my glasses on, she thought, and greeted them very warmly and cordially. From a distance. She felt completely calm and sure of herself. When you're young, you don't think you'll ever experience this sort of feeling, she thought. Like being on some sort of high plateau. Like being free, and still part of it all. Having a position. With the tiniest hint of resignation, perhaps? No, why always find negative associations—why not just plain accept that one is growing up? Finally.

While she was calmly combing her hair and perfecting the contours of her lips, she saw in the mirror that Nils was talking with his boss. And then the reflection of the wife's face appeared next to hers. They greeted each other with a handshake this time and, so, unexpectedly landed in the intimate realm of ladies' concerns. As a result, the blue-haired sixty-year-old suggested that they address each other by their first names.

She thought about this when finally settled in her orchestra seat watching the advertisements that came from the theatre's quaint old projector, and considered it a victory. She, actually, would have chosen another mirror. A little distance never hurts. A triviality. Of course! But you can never be sure. Suddenly we call each other by our first names. Two families making believe they know each other. No, I really wouldn't have...I won't do this if...when I get to that position.

There. Now she'd thought it. And it didn't seem impossible at all. Not even far off in the future. She squeezed Nils' arm. He looked up from the program and smiled, a little surprised.

"It's just that I'm so happy," she said.

"I can see that," he said. "You do look sweet!"

"You too," she complimented him. "You really look good in that dark-blue suit."

"But at first you didn't like it! But that of course was because you hadn't been along to choose it!"

"My goodness, do you really think I'm that hungry for power?" She tilted her head and hoped that her smile would melt the pattern of frosty sarcasm around his eyes.

"Darling!" was all he said. Whatever he meant by that.

She didn't bother to think about it. That too was something that had come with having grown up. Accepting him as he was. Instead of turning him inside out, twisting and examining every word, analyzing his every mood. She leaned lightly against his shoulder and read: Scenery...producer...costumes...Olga... Irina...Masha...Baron Tuzenbach...

She had just come to the end of the long list of names when the lights went out. There was a sound of crackling in a wire as they pulled the white advertisement screen up to the dark upper regions of the theatre. The red lights at the exits shimmered mysteriously against the velvet of the draperies. She felt the same feeling of excited expectation she had felt the very first time. *Little Peter's Voyage*...or *Little Red Riding Hood*?

In this darkness where all whispers were smothered and coughs were muffled, one could now hear the curtain rustle over the stage like an enormous skirt. The stage had opened its big Cyclops eye and was staring at them. She returned the look with curiosity but now without excitement. Through her glasses.

The first act went surprisingly fast. She didn't feel like meeting the boss and his wife. She didn't want to wear out that shiny brand-new intimacy. Nils and she froze for a while in the outer lobby and smoked the same cigarette. They argued about the little blonde debutante who was playing Irina. But when she realized that Nils was upset and quite serious about it all, she smiled and gave in.

I know what my opinion is, she thought. Therefore I don't always have to say it. I can keep it to myself now in order not to spoil the atmosphere.

When they realized that the lobby behind them was emptying, they hurried in. Perhaps I spoil something by being so compliant, it occurred to her. And then the curtain went up again.

She continued to reflect a while about being so compliant and being obstinate. She should be able to be herself without becoming aggressive. But what about Nils—could he? Women were always being told that they were aggressive in discussions and conversations. She supposed it was the oppression of all the previous centuries that was now boiling over and suddenly throwing the lid off their pot of opinions. But then, could people live together and be so outspoken with each other? Didn't one of the two always have to give in? She supposed that you simply had to find areas where it didn't matter so much if you gave in. Nils lets me take care of the household exactly the way I want to.

She tried to get back into the warm pleasing theatre atmosphere of the first act. But it was impossible. A

flood of misery washed over her from the stage. It was like melted snow rushing down a mountain. She felt uneasy, and a great chill ran down her spine. As soon as we get home we'll light the candles, she told herself. And the fire! We'll light a fire in the fireplace too!
But it was too far off. It didn't warm her.
Oh, won't they ever get to Moscow, she was thinking. And then there was another intermission.
This time they got together with the boss and his wife. It would have looked strange, after all, if they had tried to avoid them. Together as a foursome they looked rather odd there in the crowd. The boss and his wife were short, in their sixties, and quite plump. As a matter of fact, they were conspicuously petty bourgeois, both in their shapes and in their choice of clothes — that is, except for her blue-tinted hair. In that mirrored promenade, where so many young couples were showing off their elegant evening outfits, they looked almost ridiculously out of place. It occurred to her that if one didn't know how important they were one would think that they were shopkeepers from South Stockholm, who had suddenly developed an appetite for culture.
"You look a little pale," the boss's wife said in a motherly way. Afraid that her sarcastic thoughts would show, she became very friendly and attentive, joining in the conversation with great zeal. Until the bell interrupted them. As a result, she didn't have a chance to get any juice.
That was too bad, because the third act made her thirsty. Her throat was dry and she felt chilly. Maybe I'm getting sick, she thought. But that would be ridiculous. I got my influenza shot only last Friday. And on Sunday we're having our big party. I just can't get sick.

She sat up in her seat. My God! Every human being knows that they'll never get to Moscow! She was really tired of the whole thing. Then she reprimanded herself: How can I be so stupid! Nothing but excuses. Desperation. Recklessness. Nonsense.

Nils was completely absorbed in the play. He could lose himself in everything. Absolutely everything. Even weeding in the garden. Or filling out income tax forms. Or improving his company's sales organization. He was so full of concentrated vitality. But, despite it all, he could give an impression of being dull and slow. But that was just on the outside.

She looked at him tenderly and thought about the shellfish au gratin that was ready to be put in the oven. And the flowers, and the candles. But it was the second time she was doing this. "Pleasures are like poppies spread: you seize the flow'r, its bloom is shed." She'd read that somewhere. And then there's just everyday reality left. What's wrong with reality. Is it something one has to cover up with flowers?

Stupid question. Is or isn't... Nobody knows what it really is like. And every human being could change that "is." A little bit at least.

And even if they do reach Moscow, Masha'll never be able to go along! Even IF happiness comes to them, it'll be gone a moment later. Myths. Just myths everywhere. Flowers. Rust-red candles. As though dipped in blood.

She looked at her watch. It gleamed, ghost-like, at her from the fold of her silk dress. But she never saw what it said. Three rows behind them somebody got up and walked quickly and noisily towards the exit. She turned around and just managed to see how he had stepped out of the row and collapsed on the floor very near the door. He no longer looked like a human being now, only a spot of deeper darkness.

No one seemed to have noticed anything! She turned towards Nils, but he put up his hand, signaling that he didn't want to be disturbed. He apparently hadn't heard anything. She twisted around in her seat again and thought she'd get up and follow the man, but saw two doormen already bent over him. He was lying there like a heavy heap on the red carpet. Completely motionless. Horrible wheezing sounds were coming from him.

She turned towards Nils again and saw his face white in the reflection from the stage lighting. It made him look alien and unreachable. When she twisted around again, the carpet was empty and the door towards the lobby was just closing with a slow plushy swish.

"What did you want?" Nils whispered.

"Nothing," she said. "Nothing important."

"And they never do get to Moscow. It really is too sad!"

"Did the play make you unhappy, or are you just joking?" he asked.

"It did make me a little sad. Although I knew all the time that they'd never get to Moscow. By the way, did they get their tea at least?"

She went on chattering to get away from that awful atmosphere of a little while ago. People were crowding and pushing, trying to get to their coats. Someone among all of these people must have sat close enough to know what really had happened, she was thinking. But no matter how much she searched their faces, she could only see that they wanted to get their coats and to get out.

"Here! Here I am! Darling, are you dreaming?"
"Yes, I guess my thoughts are in Moscow!" She smiled.
"And I was thinking about Russian tea. Shall we have some nice hot tea when we get home?"
"Mmm." She nodded, and wrapped her shawl around her head.
Near the exit they were separated. She heard an older man say to one of the doormen: "Terrible...he was lying there completely motionless..." And she also picked up a bit of the answer: "...already when we got to him."
What was it that had happened already when they got to him? Was he dead? If he'd only lost consciousness, the doorman wouldn't have expressed himself in that way, would he?
They walked through the frosty dark streets. People hurried by with turned-up collars. A couple of girls with red frostbitten nylon-clad legs and great big huddled fur animals on their heads were stamping their feet and shivering in front of a shop window. Nils was talking and laughing. This was the third time he'd seen the play. He was comparing productions. He came out with intelligent statements about Chekhov. Mentioned Ibsen, fin de siècle atmosphere. Söderberg. Hallström. Everything he said could be printed in a literary magazine. Oh, she did admire him so very much! And, at the same time, wished he would stop talking.
"...already when we got to him," echoed in her head.
He stumbles out of the row and feels his chest getting tight, the effort of his heart pumping, irregularly, and now...now he is thinking, I hope I can make it

out! All the time he is thinking that it is just one of his many attacks. I hope I can make it out to the lobby. Take my medicine. A glass of water. Calm down. Then go in again and see...the end.

Maybe that's the last thing he has a chance to think. The end. Then some inarticulate wheezing comes out of his mouth while he is already far away. And he is carried out like an object. Like the object he is. Now. But a short while ago...

"...already when we got to him."

"Darling! You aren't even listening! Where is my capable discussion partner tonight!"

"In Moscow!" she said, and felt annoyed about her stale repetition. I have to find something better next time, she thought. In a few years I won't be able to serve a stupidity together with a smile and hope that people will think me witty.

In the elevator she hid her face against his chest, and he hugged her hard, very hard. He didn't have to worry because he knew that their neighbors rarely left their apartment at so late an hour. She was glad it was so late.

Now they would light candles. Take out a bottle of wine. Yes, that's what she wanted. No matter how much he would insist on tea. It was his birthday, after all!

"But darling! So lovely! And flowers even! How nice of you!"

She heard the words, exactly as she had imagined them in the car. It seemed a very long time ago. She came in from the kitchen in order to admire her creation herself, together with him. But he had already gone into the study, and she heard him whistle while he was changing into his slippers, and she stood there and said to herself: "It is perfect. All of those rust-red colored things, and the bright-blue... no, deep-blue vase. I love colored glass. It's the newest thing. Everything used to be ceramics and stoneware. Monday I'll go out and buy something made of red glass. Anything. As long as it's red. And glass. It'll be a present to myself." All this she was thinking, and went back into the kitchen.

"Cheers!"

"Cheers, darling. And happy birthday!"

"This is the best birthday I ever had. This year," he said, and smiled with his whole face. "That shellfish au gratin was perfect! And the table! And you! And everything!"

When she had taken her bath, he was already in bed. She stretched out next to him and knocked the book out of his hands.

"Don't do that!" he said, but then he smiled and passed his hand over her face and hair absent-mindedly.

Now someone was perhaps wondering why a middle-aged man, a father, or son, or a friend, hadn't come home from the theatre. The play had to be over now, someone was thinking, while checking the time. And just then the telephone rang. A voice said that it was all over. "Because already when they got to him..."

"This has been a perfect day," he said absent-mindedly. And then he put his book away, turned towards her, and fumbled along her throat with his lips, and bit her shoulder gently right through her thin negligee.

"Don't worry, you can bite—I won't break," she was thinking, almost spitefully. I'm made of ligaments, flesh and blood. I am alive and solid. I never, never want to be a heap that someone carries away and..."

Angry tears were choking her, but he misunderstood her emotion and lay down heavily on top of her, and she clung tightly to him, very tightly, to keep him from feeling that she wasn't at all with him.

Much later, when waves of blood had washed them back and forth like shipwrecks over the soft beach of the double bed, he remained inside her, full of vitality for a long time.

But suddenly all she wanted was to know about what had happened to the other one, the stranger, already when they got to him. Perhaps she should return to the theatre tomorrow? Make enquiries? Her very existence seemed to depend on whether he was alive or...

Oh, she would never find out. Oh, death got hold of people in this way every second of the day. In the whole world. He was groping for her already, and her senses would leave her, her glass objects would betray her, and the colors would fade, and darkness would swallow her... And he was lying like a heap on the dusty carpet, where they all sat wearing their evening shoes. And those whom he had just stumbled by were staring with pale faces into the big shining eye of the stage. While he...excluded from their community was lying like a heap of clothes, and deep inside him there was something half strangled trying to make itself heard, trying to leave a last message, to call for help... Oh!

Her scream was long and violent and desperate. But he understood it to be the signal he had been waiting for... "You are perfect, darling," he whispered in her ear.

The King Is Threatened

THEY RECOGNIZED EACH OTHER immediately across the pistachio-green lobby.

Recognizing each other couldn't really be taken entirely for granted: the majority of their colleagues here had trouble with both their eyesight and their memory, and it happened that the same old ladies or gentlemen introduced themselves anew around the breakfast table every day, not being at all aware of having breakfasted with more or less the same people for years.

More or less, that is, since departures as a result of natural causes were many. If one moved to a boarding house, or whatever one wanted to call the place, in one's eighties, one couldn't really expect to stay so very many years. Not even in this sort of a place. No, it wasn't a nursing home. If the boarders got too sick, they were transferred to other institutions, and dispersed, each to his own district.

Maud and Charles, however, had been friends on the outside. Through the years they had played bridge together in different places, eaten luxurious meals, talked about each other's children and grandchildren, yes, even sat around the same Christmas tree once in a while, and retired with a yawn to have drinks when they could no longer tolerate the children's and young people's rustling with the wrapping paper, followed by their spoiled comments.

Maud's father had been a cousin of Charles' mother's. But it wasn't just that distant relationship, it was also the fact that they had spent their summers near each other that had created special ties between them and between their families.

In Charles' case, it had been his wife who had persuaded him to take lodgings "for a while" as she put it, "at least two months," she had added, at Waybridge Manor. Maud, on the other hand, had made the decision herself, had moved in a few weeks before, and could now show Charles around. She had already become the habitué, she knew everyone and was so bright and capable that many wondered enviously why she was there at all, and there was actually a rumor that she was some sort of a spy from the world of the young and healthy, the world of the sexagenarians, or else, that she'd been smuggled in because she knew someone on the board of directors.

It was worse for poor Charles. He was a clear case for Waybridge. He sat mostly in his wheelchair. He could only manage to walk a few steps with the help of a supporting arm and a crutch. These steps were rationed for use between his bed and the bathroom, and between the wheelchair parking place outside the dining room and the table near the window. Exhausted and white in the face, he would collapse in a chair, and absentmindedly scatter thanks around—a sort of rigmarole that always ended with: "Imagine ending up like this!" And it was said with genuine astonishment.

If it was Maud who had helped him, which often was the case, she would pass her hand lightly over his sparse white hair, and in a motherly tone say: "We're old, all of us." Or else she'd say: "Lots of people are worse off, don't forget, Charles!"

That sort of expression flourished inside Waybridge. Situated as it was, on a hill near a bend in the river Way, it actually looked more like a sanitarium than a manor. This despite the fact that its exterior had not at all been altered since the time when Lord Southey, a destitute bachelor, had sold it to a foundation called "Care of the Aged" at the beginning of the 1930's. (After concluding the sale, the Lord went on a long dreamed about journey around the world, got stuck in Hong Kong when the war broke out, and disappeared among that city's tumultuous millions.)

It was as though the architect at the beginning of the nineteenth century had foreseen the future destiny of his building. There was something impersonal, pompous about its low broad crenelated tower, the bare, flat avenue leading to the entrance, with the harshly pruned poplars, and there was something decidedly unfriendly about its steep northern slope down to the river. A Russian boarder once had called it "the precipice" because it reminded him of a novel by Goncharov, and it has kept that name ever since.

Along the edge of the precipice, there were some donated park benches that bore silent greetings from former boarders on brass plates. "Mrs. Williamson's bench, where she often used to enjoy the view," soon became Maud and Charles' private bench. The nearby little woods contained hundreds of song birds, and if you managed to get away from your talkative neighbors, you could listen to redstarts, spotted flycatchers, yellow buntings and blackbirds here. With "the place" behind your back, you were spared its ugliness and could for a short while feel like a free human being on an excursion in nature.

Without thinking about the additional trouble, Maud would on those occasions help Charles get out of the wheelchair, and she would wheel it a bit out of the way, so that he could be spared the sight of "that dreadful contraption." He hadn't needed to ask her, she had intuitively thought of these small gestures and considerations which made him feel younger, healthier and even more manly.

Not like with Christabel, Charles couldn't keep from thinking. She would, instead, call attention to all that was belittling and derogatory in his present situation. Present, well, he was neither ignorant nor afraid, he realized that this "present" was permanent, sort of a terminal station.

"At your age you don't have to worry about that," she had answered one time when he had in vain tried to remember the origin of the word "scarlet."

"Woman," he had wanted to shout while thumping the floor with his cane spasmodically, "do you happen to know that you are speaking to an old etymologist?" But for some unknown reason, he had come out with entomologist—thus mixed up a linguistic scientist with an insect scientist, just as he had done as a schoolboy. It was incomprehensible because he had spent his whole adult life with etymology, and that mixup had already caused him so much embarrassment when he was twelve, when it had been especially mortifying, since it had happened in connection with his Eton entrance exam.

With an enormous effort he had later taken down the proper volume of the *Encyclopaedia Britannica* and greatly enjoyed refreshing his memory about the little scale insect which when dried produces such beautiful shades of red when mixed with stannous chloride. Comes from the Persian: saqirlat. And in his delight about the correctness in his unintentional mixing of linguistic scientist and insect scientist, of etymo and entomo, he muddled through an explanation, interrupted constantly by paroxysms of laughter, which made Christabel only shake her head like an idiot. Most likely she called the directress at Waybridge Manor for the first time on that particular evening.

He wondered quite a while whether he should tell Maud all about it, about Christabel, the scale insect and the encyclopedia (why, for God's sake, didn't the woman place his favorite books closer to the floor so that he could reach them from his wheelchair, instead of having to use the, to him now impossible, library ladder?), but he was overcome with so much disgust just thinking about Christabel's small meannesses that he decided to devote his attention to the singing of the birds, and, almost distractedly (as though he was looking for the handle of his crutch), he put his hand on Maud's knee, and she let it stay there.

The two old people had already spent more than a week at Waybridge before the relatives realized that the other one was there as well: that is, Christabel discovered during her Sunday visit that Aunt Maud was one of the boarders, and Maud's granddaughter Diana saw to her delight that it was Uncle Charles, who sat as close as possible to the sofa when afternoon tea was served in the lobby.

Later, when they strolled across the gravel court towards the parking area behind the gardener's place (where the ground was always soaked by hoses, which made all Waybridge visitors take along special boots or overshoes), they both loudly asserted their delight about the fact that the two old people could enjoy each other's company.

"It could become awfully boring otherwise," Diana said, and cast a glance over her shoulder at the pale gray walls with their pompous puffy stucco ornaments that looked as though made of whipped cream, and the obviously false mediaeval towers. "Grandmother asked me to bring along her chess set next time I come to visit."

"An excellent idea," said Christabel, but added: "However, I doubt whether Charles remembers the rules of the game. He can't manage so much nowadays."

Then, they talked a bit about boarding fees, and about prices of things in general, and when they took leave of each other Christabel said: "Perhaps, dear Diana, you think me heartless, but it feels so good to be able to rest a while. You can't imagine how good it feels." And, Diana, who lived alone, could very well imagine, but at the same time she thought that it would be inspiring to have an old Charles to talk with when the television got tiresome, and the dark of the night pressed against the window panes.

* * *

"Wasn't it sweet of Diana to send me the chess set?" Maud said gaily a couple of days later. Charles, who very well remembered that Maud explicitly had asked her granddaughter to send it, wondered over this unsought opportunity to make of this a special thing to be grateful for, when it really was a matter of course. Perhaps this was the way one "fixed up" one's existence as Christabel ill-humoredly used to say. "She's one of those people who fix up everything so that you won't be able to see how gray it actually is." But what is there actually? he wondered as he rolled himself closer to the table where Maud was already setting up the pieces. "I mean, what is there actually deep inside?" And he was glad that he hadn't tried to express himself aloud.

"Do you want us to throw dice for white or black?" she was wondering now, but he immediately said with a ready wit that amazed him: "You may be my white lady, dear Maud," and she smiled her quick smile and turned the board around so that he could play black.

"Such beautiful pieces," he said to gain a little time. It was a long time since he had played and he was searching inside his head for the layers and drawers in which chess knowledge had been packed away. If these archives were moth-eaten he would be lost. But there, as clear as small glass pearls in crystal-clear mineral water, words came to him like gambit, castle, stalemate and j'adoube.

"We bought them in Cairo. Edward and I," Maud said. "It was a long time after he retired from his post there. We were just on vacation."

Since they were sitting in the big lounge with its electric fire in the fireplace and all of the cozy groups of soft armchairs and little tables that were much too low, the word Cairo made another old lady look up. And she said, very loudly to her friend, because they were both deaf: "Cairo! Oh, do you remember? It's a sunken paradise now. It doesn't exist anymore!" "What did you say? Cairo doesn't exist?" the friend, who hadn't read the newspaper for many days, inquired. "Oh, it's gone, gone. Just like Rhodesia. Rhodesia doesn't exist either. Only those—those barbarians!"

Maud was about to exchange an ironic smile of mutual understanding with her chess partner, but Charles had obviously not heard a word of their neighbors' conversation.

"Another time we can sit in my room and play, Charles—," she said gently. "It is quieter there." But she wasn't even sure that Charles had heard her nearby voice. He was hesitatingly fingering his black horse, and was thinking so hard that his forehead became lined like music paper.

Maud's room was somewhat larger than Charles', as a matter of fact it was larger than all the others on that corridor. Neighbors, who at some time had come to visit her, had found that fact just as suspicious as her vigor and good health, and instead of having become a center for social activities of her choice, as she had hoped when she had seen that there was room enough for a coffee table and easy chairs, the room had contributed to her being shut out.

God knows, there weren't so many you could associate with. There weren't many with an intact memory and some sort of vitality in their legs or in their wits, and she wasn't especially interested in some of those arch-reactionary memories. She didn't belong to those who considered "Rhodesia" or for that matter the rest of Africa to be a sunken Atlantis. She read her *Observer* every week and telephoned Diana at least every other day and, sometimes, although remarkably seldom, she called Charles' wife, Christabel.

"Thank you," Christabel would say, somewhat on guard, "I am in contact with him myself, so you don't have to report on him, dear Maud."

But rather than feeling snubbed, Maud then became even more cordial and agreeable and she felt that it was only now, when she had Charles more or less in her care, that she really began to understand Christabel as well.

"Nothing wrong with my wife, really, you can't say other than good when it comes to women," Charles said, "but she is a cold woman. Really cold, Maud." They were sitting in easy chairs in Maud's room, and since the coffee table was so rickety and so little that it could only hold the chess board, Charles had to support himself with one hand on Maud's knee when he leaned forward over the game. "Please excuse me," he mumbled, but Maud pretended not to hear him. Nor did she take his hand away from her knee.

And when she went to bed that night, in the high resilient bed with the many thin blankets in layers to ward off the humidity which the night wind blew into the room, she passed her hand over that same knee, that still soft and rounded knee, and she felt that it was warmer than the other one.

"Diana," Christabel's voice said unexpectedly on the phone one early morning. "I'm sorry to bother you, but I have to ask you something about Waybridge. It seems to me that Charles isn't getting such good care there. What about Maud?"

"Well, Maud is so hearty and chipper," Diana said. "It really isn't a question of 'care' in her case...so, it's difficult to compare, I think. I thought Charles was getting diathermic treatments. And vitamin shots—have they stopped those?"

"Oh shots, shots, shots," Christabel chattered like an angry blackbird, "they think that helps! What he needs is massage. And help in walking with his crutches. The way things are now, I suppose he'll be sitting in his wheelchair until he won't be able to take a single step by himself, I mean, he just isn't getting the kind of care he gets at home."

"But I thought you needed a rest," Diana said unwittingly. "You did seem tired of waiting on him—but then, that's natural," she added, for the very silence seemed negatively charged.

"Tired of Charles..."

"I didn't say that, Christabel..."

"No, but tired of taking care of him then. Of course not! How can you possibly believe anything like that? Has Maud intimated anything of that sort?"

"Not at all. On the contrary, I think our two old people enjoy each other very much. They really take care of each other. Last time I called, Maud said she didn't have time to talk because Charles was sitting in her room having tea. She's got permission to have one of those instant tea makers in her room, you know, and what's more, she goes to the village to buy scones. She really sounded unusually bright!"

On that very same day Christabel called the directress at Waybridge and asked whether Charles could come home for a few days. She said that it was her birthday, as a pretext, but Charles, who suddenly seemed to remember almost everything, said that it certainly wasn't, and that he was well off where he was. And the directress thought that he sounded resentful.

At any rate, Christabel came to pick him up. She seemed very rested and managed to get him and the wheelchair into the car by herself. But when they got home, only the first evening had any trace of welcome celebration, and as a result Charles ate too much, got indigestion and had to spend the night in the bathroom in his wheelchair, in order to be near the necessary conveniences.

On the next day both he and Christabel were tired and washed out. Charles was yearning for the copy of *Broca's Brain* which he had left half finished in his room at Waybridge, and at teatime he complained that the tea was too strong, and asked where the chess set was.

Christabel took it down from the highest shelf in the library, and then he sat in the dusk, fingering the pieces that he had set up, knowing very well that Christabel didn't know how to play.

It was a gray wet day in March. The naked branches were shiny in the rain. A robin redbreast twittered hectically outside the window as though trying to hasten the arrival of spring. A blackbird raced back and forth between the arborvitae and the snowberry bush like a harassed black spirit. Nature outside was restless and contrasted strangely with the stuffy quiet inside where the hissing of the radiators was the only sound. When Christabel called that dinner was ready, there was no answer. She found Charles in his wheelchair which he had rolled to the telephone table in the hall, and she heard him say in an odd low voice: "Just leave the pieces as they were, Maud. Don't touch them. I'm coming back."

It was a very silent dinner and Charles blamed his lack of appetite on the events of the previous night. On the next day he insisted on being taken back to Waybridge, and Christabel granted his wish with mixed feelings of anxiety and relief. Already in the lobby, Maud came towards them with rouged cheeks and sparkling eyes. "There's our old darling," she shouted and hugged first Charles, then Christabel who chewed on that "our" all the way home in the car and understood that she, for the first time in her thirty-five-year-old marriage, shared her husband with another woman. Was that proper? she wondered and felt that she was blushing and almost drove through a red light.

"Diana?" said Christabel's voice early the next morning. "Diana, do you hear me? It's such a bad connection... well, listen, you'll have to excuse me but isn't it just a little too much, this business with Maud and Charles? Don't get me wrong, I'm not jealous, one doesn't get jealous at my age, and especially not with an old man like Charles who can't really do anything anymore, poor darling..." Here, she interrupted herself and giggled because she realized too late that "can't do anything anymore" was rather insinuating and, what's more, she had unconsciously called him "darling," just as Maud had.

While Diana was trying to help Christabel across

these new and never-charted deep waters, Charles and Maud were sitting very close together with their chess board.

"I had such a strange dream last night," Charles said and cleared his throat. "I mean such a wonderful dream." Maud's gray eyes looked at him intently. Her white hair surrounded her forehead like a curly halo, but there wasn't any cool saintliness about her.

"I dreamed that I was standing on a black carpet that was completely square, and that I couldn't move. I remember that I was thinking that the wheelchair was far away, off the board. It was then that I realized that the black carpet was a chess square. And then, don't laugh now, dear Maud, after all, we are a couple of old and experienced people, and..." But he couldn't continue, and his eyes, which seemed least of all old and experienced, looked entreatingly at Maud.

In the corridor you could hear the sound of shuffling feet and high shrieking voices. A food wagon clattered by on its way to someone who had become bedridden and could not be part of the eating circle downstairs for a long time. Their eyes continued to look at each other with a timeless and mutual thirst.

"What happened then in your dream?" Maud urged him to continue.

"The white queen came towards me. And I was the black king. The pawns stepped aside, and the bishop ran away. A horse put out his hoof to trip her and laughed horribly, showing his big, yellow false teeth. I can't understand how I knew that they were false teeth, but you know what dreams are like, don't you! And the white queen just continued striding towards me. I have to get away from here, I thought, otherwise

I'll be taken. And then, well, then I saw that the white queen was you, Maud. And I stood completely still. Completely still, I was only trembling, and then I took a step towards you." During the following month Christabel sent for her husband again and again. He must come home. Perhaps for good? He must be rested by now; she was, at any rate, she said in a tense and bitter voice.

He put up with these punitive command excursions, but sat silently at her beautifully set dinner table, and behaved generally like a stranger. One day in April she found him in his wheelchair out on the terrace. He was sitting there, and with unseeing eyes was facing the blooming forsythia, while tears ran down his cheeks. Christabel sneaked back into the house and pretended not to have noticed, but his tears ran like drops of hydrochloric acid through her mind.

Charles' seeming so stimulated and happy whenever he returned to Waybridge counteracted his purposes constantly. "This isn't really the right place for you, young man," the doctor said jokingly when he made his weekly rounds among the boarders. "Blood pressure perfect. Heart and lungs the same. Nothing wrong with your memory. A slight weakness in your left knee, but that's not enough. We'll discharge you, and return you to your longing wife," he said and disappeared laughing into the corridor.

If he then, by mistake, had gone in to his patient again, he would have thought he saw an entirely different person: a broken old man, with an irregular heartbeat and higher blood pressure, who restlessly rubbed his veiny old hands, while his eyes wandered over the plaster decorations around the ceiling.

* * *

Finally it was summer. Summer, the season that was longed for and feared by all. Some of the old people would be able to "join their families in the country." Their well-intentioned children came and picked them up in clean shiny cars full of well-dressed grandchildren with white teeth and loud voices. Others were forgotten and suffered because of it. Still others felt forced to agree to a stay in the country which they secretly feared: the heat would be uncomfortable, they'd feel their age more, the children's happy good samaritan efforts would soon diminish and they would be left to boredom in someone else's garden, with only the cat as company.

Maud would of course go to her country place in Somerset, as usual. And Christabel, who had considered spitefully to let Charles stay at Waybridge all summer (now that Maud was out of the way), was forced by her conscience and by Diana's questioning eyes to take him out, which meant that he, and she, would be situated at only a ten-kilometer distance from Maud. And Maud who still rode her bicycle, and Diana who loved to drive a car!

Christabel postponed their departure as long as possible, but finally the heat and the quiet of the little suburb became too much for her as well, and she and Charles and the wheelchair drove out to their summer cottage.

Already on the second day Maud came over on her bicycle, and Christabel had to take the chess set out to the garden. From the kitchen window she could see them sitting very close to each other. Charles' almost bald head, and Maud's white hair halo, which, al-

though very thin against the light, made quite a contrast against the bougainvillea that grew up the wall behind them.
For a moment she liked what she saw. They radiated a sort of peace that she did not share. A couple of pieces had found their places—but it wasn't her puzzle. She liked what she saw and at the same time she didn't. Something was tormenting her inside, and she refused to give it a name.
Then there were other days with more company. All mixed, children with grandchildren, relatives with relatives. And then both peace and tension were dispelled and Christabel said to Charles that it was a very nice summer, wasn't it? And sometimes Charles smiled at her and took her hand and said: "Yes, dear Christabel, I'm so well off!"
But when fall came, and he was silent and listless in his wheelchair and almost refused to eat, she returned him reluctantly to Waybridge, and when on the first Sunday in September she came for a visit, something happened. She opened the door to Charles' room, and, since he wasn't there, she immediately went across the corridor to Maud's room and opened that door as well, without knocking.
What she saw alarmed her at first from the point of view of Charles' health. She thought that he had had a stroke. Otherwise, why should he lie, as though unconscious, straight across Maud's easy chair, with such a stupidly open mouth, and showing mostly the whites of his eyes? The next moment her jealousy, quite rightly, got the upper hand, and she screamed a rather dirty word, went out and slammed the door with a bang.
It didn't take long for Maud to catch up with her

on the wide staircase down to the lobby. "For God's sake Christabel, what is the matter?"

"There's nothing wrong with me. You're the one who's crazy, Maud. Man crazy! Can't you leave old Charles in peace? Don't you understand that you can kill him that way? If he gets worse he can't stay here, you know. I'll be the one to have to take care of him... I mean, of course I'll do it gladly, but not if it's a result of his... and your... and it's dirty! That's what it is: dirty! And dangerous, as a matter of fact!"

She sounded furious and bitter, like a schoolgirl who had seen a friend juggle with her favorite ornament: a cat made of thin gold-plated porcelain.

"But please," Maud said, and smoothed down her hair. Her cheeks were very flushed. "Please, Christabel. I am old. And Charles is old. And—" She didn't say: you are too, but she paused long enough for those words. "Do we really have to take it this way?"

They sat down in a couple of the deep easy chairs in the lobby, and were silent for a long time. Christabel whimpered now and then. Finally Maud began to speak. She spoke quietly and with a lot of tenderness. She put one hand on Christabel's arm, and Christabel let it stay there. After about an hour they got up, and Christabel said: "Well, the most important thing is that he doesn't find out that it was me. I feel so ridiculous." And Maud lied: "No, of course not. He was sleeping, the old darling. I told him that one of the personnel had made a mistake." And: "You're careful with him, aren't you? He is all I have," Christabel whimpered. "Besides," and there was a spiteful schoolgirl tone in her voice, "besides, I'm going to take him home as soon as I get the wheelchair ramp built."

"When will that be?" Maud asked innocently.

"Hard to say," Christabel said nonchalantly. "It isn't easy to get workers nowadays." And the conversation turned into a general condemnation of workers, wages and labor unions.

One of the old ladies in another deep, flowery easy chair, picked up the word "socialist" and burst out: "And Rhodesia is gone! Gone for ever!"

When they said goodbye at the car, Christabel had almost started to believe that Charles had actually fallen forward in his sleep. But as soon as she had started the car and driven out towards the main road she hissed: "I did see what I saw!" and she stepped so hard on the accelerator that she only narrowly escaped hitting a young Arab at the crossing.

Maud walked across the lawn whistling to herself and dexterously avoided stepping on the "No Trespassing" sign. She walked as she did when she was a girl. She was thinking about an episode, a classic episode, in the lives of the Bloomsbury set when Lytton Strachey pointed at Vanessa Bell's skirt and said in his squeaky voice: "What do I see there? Isn't that semen?"

Semen, she mumbled. The chestnuts were more yellow than the sunshine. The traffic hummed like the summer's last bumblebee. A spot was congealing on her skirt, it was as big as a halfpenny.

Balzac's Valet

And for all that enormous amount of work, who'll I get? Let's see...the paperhanger, the plasterer, and the silk-weaver on Thursday. Barely time to sit down and catch my breath...whew! No, stop! Can't sit on that gilt chair with its silken seat. It's delicate as frost. My fingers would fray it, so rough they've become from scraping all those floors. Oh, well, nobody'll see, if I sit down for a minute. Except possibly the old madam. Where was I...ah yes, the flower pots from Versailles. Then the glazier, the curtain manufacturer, and the gardener on Friday. Her eyes are so sharp that with her spectacles on she can see around corners, the master said. I've noticed it myself.

But he, he's out of reach. Far away from here. Bedded down on the Russian steppe, I heard. With rugs and furs and women. That is, the woman. Just wonder who's... François!!! Get me a warm toddy! Come here with a shoehorn! Take out the silk coat with the gold tassels! And me, with the tray in one hand, candlestick in the other, I pant up the creaking spiral staircase, so out of breath I can hardly manage to stand up straight, and then... There they lay in their indecency. Susie. Lolo. Or whatever she was called. Cover the creature, I pant. Like animals... He laughed so much his stomach shook. Those were the days. Poverty and starvation. Now he's gone, with his Ukrainian. But me, I...

Why? I ask myself sometimes. It can drive you insane, as they say. The old woman watching me like a hawk. And his letters: new instructions every week. One week this, next week the other. François here, François there. Sometimes I think that he can see me in some mystical way. His black eyes pierce through me from hundreds of miles away. As soon as he can manage to lift his head from the furs and get a moment's respite from his fever, he looks straight at me. François, you didn't... François, did you again forget ... Who broke the... Who neglected to... Who... François! Answer! Yes, Sir, I said to the air, and one arm shot out automatically and hit the wall so that plaster dust whirled in the air, and I rubbed my arm to keep from getting black and blue marks, and when I looked up the old madam was standing there in the doorway staring at me so strangely...

When the mirrors came the other day, they were dusty and looked so old. That's the way they're supposed to be, the madam said sarcastically. She meant old. I went after a chamois and rubbed and polished. They looked as though death had already ravaged the place and the master and mistress had long since moved away. I stood there with the rag in my hand and saw her move through the house phantom-like, and she went up the stairs slowly and I thought she was a mourner. I'm an old vulture on the scent of disaster. So I rubbed and polished all I could to get rid of the threat of death together with the dust on the mirrors.

But still! Now in the sunshine I can see a milky film with the colors of the rainbow inside. And despite the fact that I'm alone in the house, and the madam isn't expected for hours, I can see them down there swimming around like carp in dark water. One that's big and round and black, that's the master. A goldfish with lacy fins and a sluggish tail, that's her, the Russian. The gold beckons and lures. Now he sniffs her, struts and swaggers, but without a waist he has to bow with his whole body. The black carp is at the bottom. I have to rub hard to get rid of him before they come. You can't have fish inside the mirrors. In Russia their frames are empty, I heard. Their money ran out after the gold frames. Perhaps he just pictured himself too much, and now he's only got the frame without the picture, hahaha! I'd laugh if I had the time.

Emperor-crazy! That's what I told my mother. Already out there in Versailles. The garden was nothing but gravel, very practical, but not exactly as empire-like as he had pictured... Always been crazy about mirrors. I mean gardens. This one here is big enough for a man and his pipe. You can even hear singing from the convent. That doesn't take any room! Now they can live it up! Pendules. Silks, lusters, little lamps. And eagles! Wherever I look. Bronze eagles. Gold eagles. Glass and silver eagles. The whole house is full of eagles. Perhaps he thinks he's going to barter himself to the Russian Czarship in addition to the bartered bride! Ha!

Today there was a letter again. I could tell by looking at the madam as soon as she arrived. One a day at this point. He decides the date and then he changes it. Changes the drawings. Sometimes he doesn't remember right: puts sofas in the air. Chairs where the tiled stoves are supposed to be. Hangs lamps in the trees, and puts the matrimonial bed in the chapel. I protest!

Sometimes I have so much time that I don't know how I'll have enough. Sometimes I'm in such a rush that I don't bother to do anything at all. There's no point in it, whatever I do, it's too late. I can feel it in my bones. They're most likely already on their way to Paris "marching double time." Marching! He's got the Empire on the brain. Sometimes he won't let me spend a penny. Sometimes it can cost a mint. Makes no difference if we bust the kitty, he writes. Then, a week later, I'm supposed to dismiss the carpenter, the painter, the paperhanger. And do it all myself! Of course that way it really gets done well. But, me, I'm worn out like a paintbrush with no bristles left: I scrape and chafe the walls without a drop of paint. And with a trowel so warped that all of the mortar drops on the floor. And the madam pokes around and checks on me. She gets instructions. I get orders. She gets counterorders. Sometimes we quarrel as though we were man and wife... You'd better watch out, or else...! she screamed the other day and had forgotten I hadn't been paid yet.

Then, of course, she changes her tune: Will François now please... My dear M. François, even. That's when the master has picked on her from his frigid chateau out there. The madam gets pangs of conscience. My pangs are of a different fabric. My head's full of fabrics. And eagles. Never saw a house as full of eagles as this. A regular zoo. A bronze zoo... And I'm the ape: the way I climb around. Curtains for those high windows. Lintels over the doors. Paintings up on the walls. The bedroom full of loving pairs. I'm a swallow with my mouth full of plaster. I fling myself up the walls, to the ceiling and spit out gold, silver, velvet, rags. And eagles, I'm the swallow feeding the eagles, and in the end they swallow me.

When the workmen were still here, I played boss. Sat in the middle of the floor and directed, and they had to do the running and jumping. Get going! I screamed, and they ran with their paintbrushes and pots of glue and bronze paint. I almost turned into a gold statue with only a few spots of skin still showing. I saw it in the pier glass. Like some sort of Louis statue covered with pigeon dirt. Then the plasterer plastered both the ceiling and me. Then came the order: change in plans. Purse strings pulled tighter. Out with the riffraff. Just as well. Now it'll get done right!

No, can't sit down. Today the pendule arrived. There's a bronze eagle on it. With enormous wings. For the flight of time.

And he's flying in his sleigh across Russia. Will he ever come home with his princess? What am I killing myself working for otherwise? What if he doesn't come back to this godforsaken place?

Now look madame. Look what I've managed since last: the rooms on the upper floor, the young master and mistress' bedroom suite. Mademoiselle's red room. The young count's library. All finished. But what about the stairs, said the old hag? The stairs? What do you mean? They're to be as red as the master's dressing gown. The carpet's to be rolled out. But the plasterer has to be finished first. Isn't he finished yet? the nag nagged. There's not enough money, gracious lady, I said. First the louis d'or, you know, then the curlicues ... Oh, dear. Poor woman. His letters wound her. They come from behind. Lie in wait on some corner of the table, hidden in a deep silver bowl. Suddenly they pop up and bite. Then she catches it and flies here and barks and bites me. And I can feel the words nip me in the legs and I rush around like a madman. Where was I? Blue damask? White porcelain jugs! The drawing-room chairs have to be picked up on the rue de la Seine. The carpenter's sick. The shop's closed. Back home again. And I find a note from the carpenter's apprentice who was here and couldn't get in. Such misery! A pain in the neck. Then the weaver. Lives in the outskirts. Takes the whole afternoon. My feet hurt. Home again. Dusk. And not enough lamps.

So I walk around with a candle. And I think: why not stuff these empty spaces full with fabrics, gold, bronze, eagles, so that no one can get in? Why take the trouble to dig these grottoes, in all that fabric, bronze and eagle mess? Small burrows they have to creep into and where they don't have room to turn around and have to back out with their rear ends first. Human burrows. So much trouble. Why not do like swallows: spit up some wallpaper, curtains, rugs, mahogany furniture, and smear it on the rock. Finished and done with.

Now the light from my candle falls on a big envelope. A mess of postmarks. Taken a long time to get here. Actually written before the letter I got last week. The wallpaper is to have a pattern with cupids on it.

No more stripes. He's seen that kind in a wooden castle on the steppe. Where he walks around in a sable coat and straw slippers on his feet because of the draft. Or maybe they're fur? They were straw when he sat and wrote something long and difficult, something quite unreadable that I've never looked at. And he ate the most watery soup I've ever seen. You could see the crowns on the bottom of the plates through it. And it did have to be crowns! Crowns! Eagles! They flutter up from mirrors, washstands, china cabinets, chandeliers. Shadow eagles follow me all the way into my dreams, even with the candle out.

Dirty fingers. Thought it was plaster. But it was bronze paint, made marks on the wallpaper, so, have to redo it all—but slowly. Take my time. Don't touch. Rub out marks.

I thought the madam was an eagle until I got a good look at her. She said kindly: my dear François! Rest awhile. He won't be here for a week. I don't believe her. My blood tells me there's no time. Hammering in my head. Hammering nails into my coffin.

The pendule strikes and strikes. I strike back. The only thing to do. Smashed to pieces! Redo it all? Time? No, you can't repair the weeks. A couple of seconds crunch under my shoes. Little brilliants. Can never be put together again.

Sweep it all up. Dirt drives the master crazy. Kitchen's full of dirty china, even though no one has eaten a decent meal here in months. Ugly crowns that I tried to wash away. She put them on the shelf unwashed. I'll have to do it tonight when no one can see. Grope my way to the sink in the dark. Can feel the steam on my hands. Dip every dish separately. Then rub hard

with a towel. The master'll go crazy if I don't...
Warm wine, damn it! Live it up! Live it down!
Live it out and live it in. Should I? Not that I've ever
had anybody in bed. Hahaha! I'll talk about it when I
get time. Three thousand pages. No, four thousand I'm
going to write. That'll show him.
    I leave stains every time I touch anything. As
though I were a snail leaving a trail of mucus behind.
Guess it's the bronze paint. This is supposed to be
plaster-white. Spic and span. Finished. Flowers. Saw
the list today and rushed out to buy some. Been sitting
here waiting for hours now. No carriage. The flowers
are drooping. The lilies. The daisies. The carnations.
They're dying and they stink. No carriage coming
down the street yet. Everything is ready. Every vase
full of flowers according to plan. Everything account-
ed for, measured, according to the drawings. The kinds
of flowers, the tables, the vases. It's all in the letter.
But what about him? Isn't he coming soon? I'm waiting and wilting together with the flowers.
    Daytime I struggle with ladders and eagles. Every
night I wash dishes with crowns on them. One day
this palace will shine with dreary splendor like a hollow gold tooth. And I?
    I'm still going around counting the eagles he listed.
So many books. So many eagles. And crowns... Always so much. So much clothing. So much body. So
much love, money, food, tablecloths, curtains. So
much master. I'm only a black skeleton in the corner.
The one that comes with wine. Soup. That gets a kick
in the behind. Food down the wrong way. François!
That's me. In like a shadow. Thin. Obliging. But he,
he swells and spreads out. The white table looks like a

bed with the sheet in disorder and bosoms hanging half naked and the master's stomach like bread dough under the silk coat with gold tassels that drag on the floor, and his foot stamping and I'm at the door blue in the face because of a piece of bread that got caught in my throat.

He's in gold over his head now. Drowning in it. Poor master. Soon only his shadow'll walk here. Will open windows. Close doors. Call and call. Why don't I come when he calls? In the guest suite. In the countess' apartment. In the garden. I'm not in any of those places, no matter how much he calls.

Third night now without sleep. Legs swollen. The floors should be polished again. The plaster rains on one's hair. I lift my arms to hold it up so that the ceiling won't come down... Like those men you see in town. Men of stone who hold up whole houses. They struggle like I do. In this house. Keep holding until I'm blue in the face. But I muster up my strength and lift this whole warehouse of furniture, and eagles. I attack fierce mahogany chairs. Fight rugs. Discipline draperies and strike the clocks right in their stupid white faces. Am going to hold my own against all of them until he gets here. Then: I'll put the key in his hand. Finished. All finished. I'll go away. Without anything. Without glue. Without eagles...

In my dreams I see him rush from Russia to Russia. But one day he'll leave Russia behind. Then we'll have something to see here in Paris. Rise citizens and kings! Here comes a writer in wild boar furs with his countess! I shout and cast my hat in the air, but it won't leave my fingers, they're sticky with wallpaper paste, and many will perhaps interpret my gesture as irreverence, but the master who's known me so long will look upon my great achievement and approve. On the seventh day.

I shall hear the carriage come down the street, and I shall shout: "Let there be light! The carpets will be rolled out, the bolsters turned, the tables will be set. The flowers will smell. On the seventh day, when the wedding already is a memory and only the conquest of Paris remains.

Now rags and newspapers. Off the floors! Here's the carpet for the stairs. Here the vases. Emptied. A trash pile of flowers in the kitchen garden.

Hear her poking around in the kitchen. Passing her finger over the shelves. All the porcelain is swept up. All the sweeping washed. All the washing swept. The mirrors plastered. The eagles shot. The beds varnished. The windows beaten.

The marble gleams. I'm dull. Go to the bedroom and dream of a maid. Rosy. Round. Like my mamma. Only women I've seen. My mamma. The Lord's mamma. All others only a bit of fabric, rosy or prickly or smooth. The spot that catches my eye is like a brooch. They do like brooches on their breasts, don't they?

A strange quiet today. An omen. Now. There. In through the door. I see, I can see: him, round, rolling in his red silk coat with a gold staff in his hand. Her: tall, sails after like a frigate with a sail of lace and chiffon. I'm a black hunting dog, I bow and scrape with my coattail whipping around like a double tail. He puts his big staff to my stomach and pushes it through: there I am, nailed to the wall next to the door. There I will remain forever. A valet made of wood and copper to hang one's clothes on. In whose hand you drop red-hot pipe ashes without his twitching a muscle. Ah! Water! Water! for my hand!

Today's the day. I rush around. The pendulum won't. Strike. Must strike. I strike it. The damask. Doesn't want to. I wipe it. Clean. Not a grain. Shining clean. All around. Everywhere. A draft of wind sweeps clean. Plaster from the ceiling. Must move slowly. Move carefully. Red silk coats swept along with the rest. Up to the sky. Under false eagles. The spinet out of tune.
 No. Won't think. What a pain! Everything's ready. Food. A profusion. For four thousand at least. Close my mouth. Button my buttons. Best livery. Now? No. Not yet.
 Vases? Why all those vases? It's cold. Get the coat. Too late. Now the flowers. Will they last until evening? And if not? All right, now? No.
 Lilies according to instructions. Silver lilies. Carnations of pewter. Bronze bowls and thin porcelain. I cut myself in the palm of the hand. Rub it with an oily rag. Stain the wallpaper. Cover it with a painting. As soon as I hear the carriage: I light the candles. Hurry. Now?? No.
 Now tulips. Then hyacinths. All palms dusted. Tulips, hyacinths, dust. Table's set. Beds made. Swept. Plastered. Painted. Now? Hear anything?
 Floors scraped. Grated. Drunk. Eagled. Pendulated. Crowned. That's not the way you say it... now?
 I've lit the candles. Lit up. Bronze. Crowns. Beds. Bodies. Round. Hot. People? Should I have peopled this house? No. They're coming. Some time. Me, I'm finished.

Lolo in the straw. Hot water jug? Shall I get some straw? Some heat?
The carriage. All ready. There's the noise. I sit and wait keys in hand. All that plaster instead of bronze. Quiet. Be quiet, François! Otherwise you can't hear... All right, there? No. The wallpaper whirls around. It's raining plaster. Broken glass under my feet. The eagles leave their frames and attack. Hear the carriage outside. In here eagles. Hate myself. Sitting rigidly. Without moving. Nobody harms a wooden valet. Covered with snow. Whiter and whiter. Nobody can see. Am drowning in plaster. Breathe. Have to breathe. In the end all is white and I think stark naked and white in the carriage drowned and thump and thump someone is pounding and I don't know. Don't move. Sit still... Now!

When Balzac and Madame Hanska had sent for a locksmith and had broken into the house on the rue Fortunée, they found François, the valet, immobile on a chair in the hallway. He had gone crazy. The house was in order and brilliant with light.

Hebe Laughs

WHERE SHE CRAWLED, the cracks between the floorboards were wide. Her middle finger went in easily and disappeared. Then when the maid came in heavy-footed from the dairy, the cracks closed, pinched her finger and she howled. After that she was terrified of the kitchen floor. She threw her arms and legs around wildly when anyone tried to put her down there. There was no fire in the hall, and chopped juniper brushwood lay strewn on the living-room floor. So she refused to crawl and was carried around, held firmly against Mademoiselle Roos' flat bosom.

She could have been a lively child. But she was hampered by terror and all the mangle-yellow swaddling clothes.

With Pollux' help she finally learned to walk. She took a powerful hold on a tuft of his wax-white wooly coat and trotted away on crooked legs. Her first stiff kirtle helped her even more: like a walker it held her upright. And so, one day she stood wonderingly in the kitchen, and had forgotten her fear. The sun spread golden silk over the butcher block. The broth pot was steaming, and the baking maid had one hand white with flour and the other black with soot, so the child laughed out loud. It was the second time she had made a loud sound in the kitchen. Mademoiselle Roos came running, accompanied by her wheezy cough. "Hebe, my darling, my little one, what is it?"

But everything was bathed in sunshine, and the peaceful scene was streaked by broad bands of dust from the whirling flour. A hen wandered in over the threshold and was driven out with a firm whack of the baker's paddle, like a shuttlecock. Now Hebe had already laughed twice in the same day, and laid the foundation for a good habit. Mademoiselle Roos withdrew to the spinet room.

Smiling, Hebe took a few unsteady steps and reached out towards a ray of sun. A warm, soft, fleshy arm drew her in. Admonishments breathed around her ears like gentle puffs of wind. She was placed on top of the wood shelf, out of reach of danger. Her heels drummed against the wood. One, two, one, two. Through the window she could make out, dimly as at the bottom of the sea, how the rooster strutted and brandished his comb, and when she also saw someone as little as she, who was walking back and forth with a knight's helmet made of paper and feathers on his head, a whole babbling brook of happy words burst from her mouth. "Aha, there's her brother," rumbled a voice that smelled of bread.

The next steps that were heard from inside thundered hard against the stone but were followed by a jingle-jangle laughter of spurs. A bony stiff leather jerkin, cooling metal and a breath richly spiced with herbs and tobacco embraced her. The arms were very strong and hard inside the velvet. She was hoisted dizzily towards the ceiling. Then she was carried, so fast she didn't have time to cry, through the long row of rooms, and cast into a witches' cauldron of muslin sleeves, guipure laces, and loud shouts. His hair hung down over his shoulders and was rough and woolly like Pollux' coat.

In the kitchen they were very surprised at such an unusual visit.

They danced often at Tärninge when she was young. After the large alterations on the house had been paid for, the old mistress advised giving up their plans for a modern park. Therefore the garden was still of the kitchen variety, full of tiresome apple trees and berry bushes. Hopelessly *démodé*, groaned Hebe Sofie and her friends.

But she had managed to make dear Mother agree to a summer pavilion. It stood in one corner of the cherry orchard. Of its four windows, the one facing east was yellow, the one facing west was blue, the one facing south was green, and the one facing north was red. Through the green one she had seen her brother leave for war, his velvet collar stained by her tears. The governess, who very much resembled Mademoiselle Roos, had run to her with smelling salts from the slim mother-of-pearl flask, but Hebe Sofie surprised them all when she awkwardly picked up her skirts and ran straight through the house and out the garden door to disappear crashing and sobbing in the thorny hedges and barricade herself in the summer pavilion.

Then she sat there weeping and saw her brother, as

tall and slim as she and with the same delicate complexion, ride away with a few friends. Behind them swayed the heavy coach, ominous in black leather like a coffin, heavy with the young men's necessities for life and tools for death.

When the news came that he had drowned, she saw in a dream how he had disappeared through shimmering green water, which made his face look warped and strange. In the soberness of her dream she saw a paper helmet with rooster's feathers free itself from his head and slowly, like a jellyfish, rise to the surface.

Next morning, in the sunshine behind the silk curtains, she remembered the occasion and laughed. Then she hid her unfitting expression in a cup of cocoa, and pangs of conscience gave vent to their irritation by punching her in the diaphragm. She wept with a cocoa smile on her lips.

At the Twelfth Night ball, the year she became eighteen, Carl Johan Severin Borgstjerna proposed to her in the blue parlor. They had danced together at least twenty times that winter, and every step had led them inevitably towards the deep curtsy and the graceful bow which ended so abruptly that their bodies pressed hard against each other, far from the dictates of decorum and the eyes of the governess. Their cheeks glowed like Christmas apples when they pressed them together and looked beyond the moss decorations through the window at the heavy snowflakes which slowly filled in the white hoarfrost outlines of the garden.

Behind their backs two flames leaned towards each other and burned as though with a single wick, until the double doors were thrown open by the housekeeper

who, her face contorted, announced that the Wrangels of Sätra had now arrived, and that Madame Krueger in the kitchen was inquiète about the gâteau de framboise, but that she had perhaps come at an inconvenient moment, and...hoped to be excused...if she... c'est-à-dire...
The two flames flickered and guttered.

Her first marriage melted away like an icicle in a child's hand. Its very memory was whisked away by a storm of plush, legal papers, misgivings and confinements. Sometimes she put her hands to her head where migraine had nested like a bird of prey in her high crown of hair, and wondered if it all had been a young girl's dream in a summer room intoxicated with elder blossoms. But we did dance, she told herself, and searched in the large former confectionary box covered with hand-embroidered silk. There were the rosettes she had used in cotillions, a few amateurish silhouette cutouts, and a pair of ballroom gloves, slim and transparent like gut.

Her thoughts were now occupied with the fatty business of making sausages. When she heard the word "neck," she no longer thought of chemises but of goose for dinner.

There had been a time of carefree irresponsibility that brought sorrow and gloom to many. She was one of those who, outwardly unaffected but with a heart pierced by an invisible dagger, had seen the new customs, almost as in play, kick over with a single dancing step all that was dearest to her in this world. Ensconced in the summer pavilion, she had seen her young husband dallying with the Finnish cousin who had lived at Tärninge one unfortunate summer.

One afternoon, when the clouds were heavy with rain, and the hawk screamed like a child as it dived over the hay fields, something burst inside of her, a cowardice found the courage to break free: she sobbed bitterly, then flew into a rage and, with an aching heart and tears of anguish, drove them both off the estate. The cousin looked like a tattered butterfly as she, teary-eyed and with her coiffure in disorder, threw herself into the coach.

Karl Hermann Kampf, Minister of Mines, became her new spouse. He disturbed life at Tärninge so that the years no longer had any springtimes. Only many Octobers with servants' resignations, and sweaty July days with new lives laboring into birth between her legs. Then came trips to Stockholm and purchases of furniture. Tärninge became the first estate in the region with the new-fashioned kerosene lamps. In the glow of the new light Mrs. Charlotta Kampf—as she now called herself, forgetting her childhood and springtime names—read Bremer, Harriet Beecher Stowe, Adlersparre and even worse troublemakers. But that was such a disgrace that it was admitted only within the family circle.

"You don't understand this, Karl Hermann Kampf," she said to herself aloud after an evening of arguments about the status of women. Even the loops of tobacco smoke which trailed behind him looked like an irritable, angry signature. But she had said it without malice or condescension. Only soberly thoughtful, like a farmer blaming himself for having sown on rocky ground. And there came a new motherly tenderness into her ways with her husband. A greater indifference, perhaps, which made it easier to forgive and live together.

During the last decade of his life, no sharp exchanges were heard at Tärninge. The children reproached her bitterly for her "hypocrisy." They were confused and repelled by her intellectual "dishonesty." Their father was allowed to tyrannize them unopposed as much as his dwindling faculties permitted. Soon they were gone. Out of the house. The oldest son, who after a long troglodyte existence at Uppsala University, suddenly shot up like a comet in the academic firmament, understood her at long last. Their correspondence wove a new thread of vitality into the worn-out pattern of her existence. My "outrigger canoe" she called him in her diary.

Satiated with years and parliamentary sessions, the Minister of Mines, Karl Hermann Kampf, withdrew into the shadows. Hate for his wife's libertine behavior remained a sharp thorn in his flesh, and his smile looked fierce with his new ivory-yellow dentures. With her own hands she wove him suit material in a modern herringbone pattern for his final years. The family in Finland sent picture postcards saying that the girls were having a lot of fun playing lawn tennis.

Her youngest son spelled out the pale-mauve ornate handwriting, and was crestfallen: he had thought the foreign game was called "long" tennis, and had already used the word a great deal to show off to the farmhands' children.

When she returned to Tärninge from her travels in Europe, she gazed at the dining room with astonishment. Was it she who had been living here?

Immediately after her husband's death she had set off on a journey to look around. In Germany and

France a new kind of art was flourishing, with light colors and rounded fruitlike forms. In Munich she had stayed with an old friend and correspondent. She had had a guest room as large as one of the barns at Tärninge: where daylight poured in through the window in broad swells, unhindered by the white linen curtains. Two Bavarian tapestries in brilliant red, green and black hung on the whitewashed walls.

The armchairs made her laugh at first. Then she liked their big embrace.

Her friend's paintings stood in the corridors, their face to the walls. But in the guest room hung a two-meter-high oil painting of a naked woman opening her arms towards the scarlet morning light. In the sea behind her there were small skerries and rocks, and on each one a woman, naked, free as she herself, with her arms wide open and her head proudly held high.

Hebe Sophie Charlotta, called Nanna by her new friends who had a romantic passion for all that was Nordic, blushed as she looked upon this host of new women. Would they ever reach firm ground? She remembered Fredrika Bremer's reflections in *The New World*: that in 1950 there would still be a need for a new Lucretia Mott to speak at the council meeting on behalf of freedom, peace and women's rights.

Before she left for home, she had a new dress made of plum-colored wool. It hung loosely as a dressing gown about her ample figure. For the first time since the summer when her marriage of love had ended, she felt sensual pleasure in her femininity, and regret.

Now she stood there dumbfounded, with both her bulging leather suitcases at her feet, like a pair of St. Bernards who wanted to be petted. The dining room seemed a monument to her marriage. Like a prison, it shut out all light with golden-brown draperies. Every step was muffled by dull brown carpets. When she touched the inner curtains of beige taffeta, she thought she heard the rustling of Karl Hermann's newspaper, and turned towards the oriental divan in the corner but found only the gently curving leaves of the brass smoking table, smiling yellowishly at her.

"This place has to be turned inside out," she shouted to Miss Roos, a descendant of her childhood chambermaid.

The turmoil lasted until she had installed electricity, running cold water and a sewage system at Tärninge. The funds began to run low, and she had to do some weaving to make ends meet, instead of merely to have presents for Christmas and weddings.

When the war was over, hand-woven materials came into fashion. Fighting against rheumatism and grief (her oldest son had died suddenly, still a young man of only sixty) she divided her time between the loom, which had taken over the dining room with all its rainbow-colored wools, and her writing, which she hurriedly hid between the pages of some Russian novel whenever she heard Miss Roos approaching over the telltale floorboards.

"Are the walls really seventeenth century?" a young writer on tour with his fair-complexioned fiancée asked skeptically.

"Of course they are, and I should know since I've always lived here," laughed Mistress Nanna.

The two young people, both equally tall and with broad, easy smiles, joined in her laughter. Then Miss Roos came with sloe-berry wine and cinnamon biscuits, and they sat there for a long time, sharing cakes and pleasant conversation, while the April light shone upon the bright skeins of wool.

On that day she noticed that there was time again for a few days of spring between winter and summer.

In the autumn she went to Karolinska Hospital to have her painful shoulder examined. What she had thought to be rheumatism turned out to be something worse, more difficult to diagnose. "Perhaps your heart isn't so reliable any more," the kind physician said, and tried to remove the fear from his words by looking as friendly as he could.

She walked away more slowly than usual. She had never before considered her end. She had lived her life with such assurance that she now wondered whether she had been superficial, or simply lacking in imagination, in the face of so much darkness.

Miss Roos was waiting for her at the coffee shop. They took a taxi all the way back to Tärninge. Such extravagance made all explanation superfluous. Miss Roos took care to ensure that Mistress Nanna no longer overexerted herself.

When the first frost came that year, Mistress Nanna took her customary morning walk. The stiff frozen grass crunched under her heavy walking shoes. On the way home she decided to walk through the cherry orchard. The summer pavilion stood there gaping without window panes. In a corner a few chips of ruby-colored glass shone brightly.

"Prune cherry trees," she wrote down in the diary she carried in the pocket of her suede jacket. "Remove the pavilion. Ask the writer who was here last spring. Plough up lawn." Painting, she thought afterwards.

But that would be an expensive undertaking. She peered critically at what used to be the front of Tärninge, now seldom seen, since the roads had been changed. The dull dark Dalecarlia red was powdered with hoarfrost.

The clock in the belfry over the front gable had stood still for more than a hundred years. But today something was different about it. One of the hands was missing. She bent, stiff-backed, and searched. She raked with her clumsy gloved fingers in the grass, breathing with difficulty. Went down on her knees and felt the frost melt through her tartan woolen skirt and reach her skin.

"There!" she said triumphantly and got to her feet holding the wrought-iron hand as though it were a scepter. Then she fell headlong into darkness.

She lay in bed at the furthest end of the old armory. Through open doors she could see the long sequence of rooms. In the kitchen she had toddled about when she was two. In the blue parlor next to it he had proposed. In the dining room she had presided over the stiffly mangled tablecloth, had seen the children's diffident faces, his imperious stare, the quaking of the aspic. Now the loom was there, she could dimly make it out, and the shelves still full of unwoven yarn.

She held up her hand to the sunlight, saw her pulse beating firm and precise, as if it would never tire. In swift leaps she had crossed the thresholds. Now she gasped as the juniper brushwood stuck into her chubby palms. There was Pollux's reassuring panting, his tongue, long and slack, lay lazily on her bare arm and didn't want to go back through the gate of teeth. Now someone was hugging her. Snow was falling. Her youngest child was laboring to be born. A fresh wind swept through Europe and was followed by the thunder of war. Once again. She had tried to deafen her ears to that storm. And now silence. One second more of sun. A fragile egg, balanced on the point of a needle.

The following day she asked Miss Roos to call the telephone company to move the phone. She wanted to talk with people she liked while she still could. The doctor had said that there was nothing to worry about. Most likely she had just stood up too quickly.

When the young writer called to ask whether he could buy the pavilion, she was sitting in the armchair by the window, sipping a hot toddy. She had just begun reading about Oblomov, she told him. "I remember so well when that book first came out!" "In Sweden?" "No, in Russia."

She laughed hoarsely like a friendly bird of prey. "I've also started writing my memoirs, but the publisher I talked with didn't want to put them into print. They were too incredible, he said. And I've experienced so little, really."

"By the way, why don't you come over!" she added after they had discussed the spicing of brandies, the availability of genuine crystal ware, and how many extra shots you had in croquet after going through the center hoop. "Bring your lovely fiancée with you. The sun is shining here today, and Miss Roos has baked Finnish fingers and shepherd's hats. She's good at that sort of thing! Otherwise, I'm worried about her, she's beginning to get so forgetful. But I suppose it's her age."

And again she made those hoarse wheezing sounds of irrepressible joy.

A year later, the writer showed his wife an announcement in the newspaper: "Mrs. Hebe Sophie Charlotta (Nanna) Kampf, née Döblin of Tärninge near Stockholm, is publishing the first part of her memoirs next spring under the title *Hebe Laughs*. The memoirs are in three parts and are collectively entitled *Across the Thresholds of Time*. Mrs. Kampf, who is well-known for her pioneering work as a craftswoman in Swedish textiles, was born on the family estate of Tärninge in 1685..."

"1685!" the writer's wife burst out. "What a stupid misprint!"

Then they looked at each other, their lips trembling between laughter and uncertainty.

Death's Midwives

When she lost her hair she finally began to cry. It fell out in tufts; her hands were full of it. Bewildered, she passed her hand over her head and felt its familiar shape. Her ears resisted, they bent resiliently. Her forehead felt damp, her nose more pointed. I'm going bald, she thought. And then she began to cry.

She was now sixty-four years old, and she calculated that she hadn't cried for twenty years. Not like this, she thought when she finally sat up in bed and turned the tear-drenched pillow over to the cool side. This wasn't angry crying, it was crying that came from deepest exhaustion, crying that originated from the deepest roots of sorrow. Her whole body took part, and it left her thinner and weaker, frail and broken. Anything could happen to her now. She was defenseless. She had been shaken by forces stronger than those she herself used to call upon when angry, upset or occasionally hysterical.

After a short nap she looked up at the grayish-yellow ceiling. There was a crack that looked like the

Gulf of Finland. A damp spot represented Leningrad. She had just returned from a trip and she was about forty. The museums had unwound their corridors and shown her their paintings. She was only forty then, and what was hard and painful in her stomach was, of course, the child. Turning her head now, she saw the view she had also seen then: the candy-pink high-rises and, beyond, the park with the blooming chestnuts, the green clouds of elm foliage, the yellow maple blossoms. It was all so distinct that she thought she could smell them. But she had already been deprived of fragrances a long time ago. Something was growing and pressing: would she perhaps give birth through the ear?

The walls were silent, and they listened. She had asked to be spared from a painting with two red tulips in a ceramic jug and a black book lying coquettishly askew in its bottom right corner. Sometimes she searched for the hole where the hook had been. She could see it very well after making the effort to find her glasses. It had become a nail on which to hang her thoughts. As long as I can see the hole, she thought... And then she imagined how she would in her most difficult hour fix that black dot with her eyes until she was engulfed by the millimeter-sized tunnel and finally enclosed by the wall. Like so many other struggling bodies who with one weak and trembling sigh had been devoured by those walls.

"Isn't there some tonic I can use for my hair?" she wondered when the day-nurse came. But unfortunately the nurse didn't join in the game at once, hesitating for an awful moment while smiles of pity, surprise and almost reproach passed over her familiar rosy face. The girl was too young. Wouldn't she be scared, later, when the time came?

Finally, she collected her wits and said: "Why, of course, Mrs. Malm. I can ask the doctor if you'd like."
"No, thank you, I can do it myself," she said tiredly. Her playfulness was over. First so many lies, then these ice-cold showers of truth, truth and more truth. She couldn't stand them anymore. It was too late anyway to become conditioned.

She hadn't touched herself for a long time. She remembered fruitless rubbings and ticklings, hour-long work-ups without even an echo of pleasure. Just a stubborn effort to make something happen to cause the dry lips to become damp, to feel a smile in her middle.

Now she thought of her vagina as an empty inkwell, forgotten in an uninhabited summer cottage. A pen dipping into it would splay and squeak and slide against the shiny walls and the rust-colored residue in the corners.

In moments of fright she would sometimes wind a strand of her thinning hair around her index finger and bite the knuckles of the other hand, as she had done when a child. By the white or inflamed red marks she could then, the next day, read the depth of her dread.

"It's all part of the picture," the spunky midwife had said, while pressing her stomach. It was her standing expression: it's part of the picture. Part of the picture, as well, were the swollen varicose veins, the heartburn, the water breaking too early, the unbearable pain, and finally the struggling little boy, held up by one foot, screaming and dangling, with vernix, umbilical cord and the little red sex. Part of the picture was also laughter and tears of joy and, alongside her, the newly bathed infant who with shiny eyes captured her for life.

She had felt more like someone being born than someone giving birth. She had been enclosed in the tunnel, there was no way back. When the pain pressed its utmost and she doubled up like a jackknife, and her urine sprayed all over the starched hospital gown, and the paper basin it was destined for was crushed in a hand which no longer obeyed her, then she had looked at the window. Five stories. One jump.

Now she lay in the other wing, on the same floor. But the thought of crossing the room and trying to see if she was strong enough to unlatch the window nauseated her. She wanted to save her strength. She wanted to continue. Despite the pain. And her mind laughed at this illogic, this instinct of self-preservation which was self-devastating, and her laughter turned into a grimace. There was little room for the intellect in this sorrowful business. Just as little as the other time when he was to be pressed out, caught and cut free in order finally to be able to look at her.

By means of many ingenious small movements and stratagems, she was able to get hold of her purse and to take out her diary. After the entry "K.S.," which was the name of the hospital, six weeks ago, there was nothing but empty pages. She had kept good notes before, but now it seemed completely unnecessary. In one pocket she had put the farewell letter to her son. She took it out sometimes to read it. It made her smile because it was for him, but actually she should perhaps cry since she would probably never see him again. She would change a word, add something, some sort of nonsense, something that would make him laugh. She remembered the interminable love letters to his father, the joy of writing them and reading them again and again before mailing them. The joy of awareness and of self-expression. The feeling that all was crystal-clear between them, that nothing needed to be searched for, suspected or interpreted from looks or gestures. Then, after that total, overwhelming effort, there had been a slow downhill slope, a dilution, a growing indifference which attacked both of them like a mutual consumption. By then, their son was eighteen years old, and they found no reason to pretend. They drifted apart and both forgot their love. She tried to remember how it had felt, but could only evoke the certainty of their friendship, possibly respect, and their independence from each other, which was just as complete as if they had been born in different centuries. It wasn't indifference. They kept in touch. They cared. But it was no longer necessary.

The nurses came and went. The nuisance of the rounds was diminished to the bare essentials. Mostly, she was left in peace. Sometimes she asked for sleeping pills and got them, but never many at a time. They overestimated her desire to take a shortcut.

Some of the nurse's aides were talkative. They would tell her of neighbors who didn't take off their clogs in the house, of foreigners who bought the wrong things at the supermarket, of children who complained about their mothers working. She listened, her head supported by two pillows, and tried to smile. A girl whose name was Brita lent her a turquoise chiffon scarf to cover her hair. "That looks good on you!" she beamed. But it didn't make her want to take out her mirror from the pocket of her purse.

When she was pregnant she had also been transformed into an inert being without exterior. Everything took place inside her, in her veins, in her womb, her head. She had closed her eyes to keep out the outside world and she had mumbled to the midwife: "Excuse me for closing my eyes, it seems so impolite." But she had wanted to concentrate on what was happening inside her body, and on the child struggling in the narrow tunnel.

Suddenly the oxygen mask had been pressed against her mouth. Someone had raised her head and said, "Take a deep breath, take a deep breath! Deeper still!"

And when she protested—no, no, she didn't want any help—they had answered that it wasn't for her sake, but for the child's. But this time they had fooled her. She had taken deep breaths thinking about the child, but they had only wheeled her into the intensive care unit, where she woke up with needles and tubes. Naturally, she thought, deep inside I knew that it wasn't for the sake of the child now—not now—he's more than twenty years old and needs neither my oxygen nor my blood. Still, out of sheer obedience, she had taken those deep breaths.

She leafed through the diary backwards. There. That's when it was. She made a mark with her thumbnail. That's when she breathed out of sheer obedience. Otherwise she wouldn't be here now, and her thumbnail would have been like ashes that had annoyingly fallen on a white sheet someone living near the south cemetery had hung up to dry. Not much had happened after that. She had been taken back to her room, and the lab results had become worse and worse. She knew this because she felt a tiredness that was deeper than any she had experienced in her life. A dullness, an indifference. "I'm turning to stone," she thought. "Molecules move more slowly, form different patterns.

Nothing can move me. That jump through the window is an impossibility, and soon my thinking will stop as well."

She read a little in *Memoirs of Hadrian* and wondered whether Marguerite Yourcenar was still alive or, if not, what her death had been like. When she was younger, she had been curious about death. She had never seen a relation die. Nor any death by accident. Perhaps the blood-covered man in the cigar store on Tegnér Avenue was dying, but she had had her little boy outside in the car, and had hurried off to protect him from the sight, and herself from his difficult questions.

She knew nothing of what lay ahead—just as little as she had known about childbirth when she was here before. A record with advice about relaxing was the only thing a friend had had time to give her on that day before she was hospitalized. Breathe deeply. Relax. Don't be so tense. Let your limbs go limp and loose. Perhaps she should listen to it again now?

She remembered the storm waves of her contractions. How, like at the seashore, you could see them from afar, as they mercilessly came closer. She had made herself dull, heavy and indifferent, allowed the pain to wash through her as though through someone else. And she had felt how it had "worked," how everything had opened up, how the child had come closer to his life. Never before had she been so close to death. Not her own, not a personal death. But so near the border between life and death. She had thought, quite clearly: "Now I know more about death than I did before," and all the while she had been lying there creating life.

The midwives had come and gone. Some went to

lunch. Others worked part time. And a nurse's aide had told her about her children's new teacher. About how much fun it was to watch the children relate to each other. It isn't really fun until you have two. She had thought about what it would be like to have two men. She'd had two once, and until the complications it had been lots of fun. Unusually much fun. But she hadn't been especially interested in how they related to each other.

Otherwise, she didn't think about her body more than she had to, right now. She was happy when she could urinate without a catheter. But her mouth was dry. The damp washcloth dabbing her lips was a pleasure, as was the sip of orange juice which she could wash around in her mouth and then spit out obediently. "It's like being a wine-taster," she had tried to tell the consulting physician, but her tongue wouldn't cooperate, so she had to remain silent. Why tell jokes? Was it so important for her to make a good impression? So courageous on her deathbed. "You have no idea how witty she was despite knowing she didn't have long to live!"

"I can tell this isn't your first baby, Ma'am," the nurse who shaved her pubic hair had flattered her that night in the basement where she had also had her enema and the blood tests. It was her first baby, and she had felt proud of being so composed and reasonable, so cooperative.

But wouldn't she have moaned and screamed if she had given birth lying alone in a ditch? And now, were she to lie on an Alpine slope, the victim of a plane crash with only space and death ahead...how would she behave? What would be her facial expression, what screams and curses would she address to the grass, the stones and the distant clouds? They are arranged like iron filings over the earth, the smoke-gray clouds. Each of them is filled with so many microscopic iron particles that they are forced to submit to the earth's magnetic pattern. She remembers the creation myth which she had read in its scientific version, and she remembers her great joy about these poetic facts. Maybe the earth changes its rolling rhythm when all the trees in the northern hemisphere suddenly get leaves and so offer increased resistance to the wind? And perhaps the rolling speed increases again in the fall when the branches stick up naked into the sky?

This was better than Isis and Osiris, better than Ask and Embla and Ygdrasil—or were they all equally distant from the truth, the same story in different versions?

When she was still actively alive she used to complain about each day that passed without new knowledge, new ideas. Now she wondered dully what it had all been for. It was dullness, rather than anguish. A disgusting lethargy. Even what she could manage became impossible, the very desire was cut off at the roots. She tried to remember the child, the child's father. The two bodies she had loved most. Straight shoulders, angular joints, firm jaws, looks that warmed her and gave her light. But it seemed unreal. Less real than the brown medicine bottle and the small iridescent medicine cups that one could stack in long flexible chains to rattle when there was nothing to listen to on the radio.

How long would this go on? And death, a relief? Can nothingness relieve? Relief from what?

"I have lived a good life, better than almost any I have heard of, and better than I could have hoped when I was your age," she had written in the letter. But between the lines he could perhaps read that no matter how good it had been, now in retrospect it all seemed horribly unnecessary, and so his life was unnecessary, as were the copulation which had created his little body, the labor pains and her pushing him out to life, air and his own breathing.

No, not that. To have borne him, to have succeeded in getting him out whole, that could never feel unnecessary. There was the limit to her scepticism, and she was a common she-fox, a natural female bear, an entirely genuine cat mother. The baby was in her belly and had to come out. The baby had to be licked. The baby needed milk, and tenderness and warmth, and to lie as close to her as though still inside the darkness of her belly. This was beyond what was necessary or unnecessary. It simply was. And she cherished this idea and held onto it. Sometimes she took out his picture—in it he was twelve years old, ephebically beautiful and mischievous—she would hold it for a long time in her hand and hoped to die that way.

She was in the tunnel, and there was no going back. But she wasn't put on a high iron bed, nor was she restrained, and no one listened with a stethoscope to her stomach and then said comfortingly: "I'll stay here now until it's over."

Until it's over. Then she would be two people. She had never imagined dying in childbirth. The baby kicked and wanted to come out. She had protected it for nine whole months and she wouldn't let it down during the last nine hours. And yet she had never been so close to death, since it was across that border the child had to go in order to live.

Now it was her turn. And she asked the girl Brita how long her shift was. "Until six, as usual," she said. "See you tomorrow morning!"

Tomorrow morning? No, oh no, would it take that long? But her body wanted it to take that long, and preferably a little longer.

Now, as then, flowers arrived from friends. Flowers from the child's father. They glowed with all their colors and withered. She herself glowed with fever and withered at the same time. She and the flowers were alike: cut off from their natural root systems, nourished with cold fluids which were pumped directly into the circulatory system. She saw the tulips: their stems full of water, they stretched, despite knowing that they would die. The lilac leaves didn't bother to pretend. But the five-pointed little flowers with their drop of sweet nectar in the middle bloomed one by one, and she asked a cleaning woman to give her some—yes, to pick them off, so that she could suck the little stems as she had done in the summer, long ago. She would have liked to ask the consulting physician to whistle with a lilac leaf between his thumbs, but probably he didn't know how and he was embarrassed enough as it was. And she was embarrassed herself. Confused and ashamed. How would she manage her death?

With the baby, newly bathed and dressed, in her arms, she had felt ashamed too. She had made an ironical face at his father and said: "This is like an ad for baby powder!" She had been wheeled through interminable corridors, and the little one slept in its white cocoon in her arms, his wrinkled cheek so close that she couldn't keep from caressing it. It was all so new. And her breasts which had lain so flat in their bra cups and rested in young men's hands, now they were suddenly to become troughs for the little pig who slurped and ate. She had loved nursing him and would most likely have kept on for a year if the DDT scare hadn't become so acute that mothers were warned about nursing.

I'll fall asleep, she was thinking. And when I wake up it'll be over. Nothing is working any longer. Even the pain has almost stopped. The pain has died before me. Just like my sense of smell, my hearing, my sight. I have been left behind, I am the last in my own funeral procession.

Then the older night nurse had sat down close to her bed, and had taken her hand, saying: "I'll stay now until..."

That's what it was like. Some midwives left before life came. Others stayed to keep watch. I'll stay now until you die, one body says to another. And one of them will get up, straighten her hair and go home to clean her house, do her shopping, have intercourse, weed the garden, borrow books at the library, and go through the envelopes of grocery receipts, while the other will remain. Dead still. All alone.

Then she began to talk. With her thin voice she tried to explain and disentangle. Like a child, she begged for better grades, for a longer vacation.

But the heavy-set woman in her forties took out her knitting and the lamp shone on her brown hair where a few white strands gleamed.

She tried to read by the pale glow of the night light.

"Even water is an enjoyment, and now in my illness I must partake of it sparingly. Yet even when I struggle with death, when they will mix it with the last of the bitter medicine, I will make an effort to savor its freshness on my lips."

But the book fell, and she was too tired to think about it. A harsh light fell on her closed lids. Someone pulled off the turquoise scarf, she whimpered as if in her sleep. *Memoirs of Hadrian*, a hard cultured voice said, and she understood that they were putting away her belongings. She was to suffer through the last of the contractions completely naked and almost bald.

"A hand to hold when you die," his drunken voice echoed. He was nineteen and newly graduated, the same as she. They had been hugging and drinking on the couch in her dormitory room and in her honor he had executed a death-defying balancing act outside her window.

No, no hand to hold. She hadn't wanted the child's father when the little one came. I'd rather be alone with the pains. You can come afterwards and share in the pleasure. No, no, no, it isn't for your sake, it's for mine. I'm the one who has to go through it. I want to be alone!

The bed was so wet suddenly. But when she said: "My water!" the stupid aide just came with a glass of water. She grasped for words, for memories, for signs which would be understood. It all was so new for her. She felt bewildered and uncivilized. A bitter satisfaction went through her: today had brought new knowledge, new ideas.

"There, there, take it easy!" And a broad, warm hand patted her cheek, stroked the back of her hand.

Just as before, she was their lawful prey. She remembered unknown women who patted her big, hard, pregnant belly. She had reminded them of something wonderful. What was the knitting woman beside her thinking about, now that she had come to the armhole?

"Is he all right?"

"Sure, just take it easy, you're doing fine. You're four fingers now. You're dilating just fine." A friendly Finn had his finger deep inside her and gave her a report from the life on the other side of birth.

She had hoped that he would remember and send her stocks and snapdragons. But instead the flowers had come from her colleagues at the university. What did they have to do with her giving birth?

Nosegay. Buttercup. Fleetfoot. Happy lark. Mother's little Oedi-pussycat. And she had promised they would marry soon, as soon as he got a little bit bigger. And at three months he fell asleep on top of her in a wide bouncing bed in England, she also fell asleep and dreamed that he was inside her, but only with his tiny little penis, and it was a sweet, happy union, very far from incest and pornography. And yet, she hadn't been able to tell anyone about it.

The queer knitting woman stuck her needles into her, one after the other, purl one, knit one, and the knit one's had barbs. She turned slowly to her side, but there were new tubes that got in the way. A voice echoed in a loudspeaker and footsteps ran. Footsteps ran away with young bodies, away from her immobility.

At last she worked herself to the surface, she had dived too deeply from the cliff into the black water. Her mother and father smiled at her in their blue bathing robes and the rock smelled like sunshine and tanned skin. Her whole body shivered, and she had blue gooseflesh. They had to rub her warm, but she continued to shiver.

Then, she was suddenly sitting in a back yard. The book on her lap was *Memoirs of Hadrian*. An oak spread its greenery over her like a parasol. Through an open window she heard his voice. It prattled and babbled, it expounded and explained. And he couldn't say "s." She made an effort to stretch her neck and look up. The sun shone in through the window. The chestnuts on the horizon bowed to an imperceptible breeze. Their scent did not reach her. The knitting woman had fallen asleep. The light hit the shiny intravenous bottle, which reflected blindingly.

All she saw was the sunshine bouncing against the nursery window, and his voice babbled on, and when she made an effort to somehow see his face the sun struck her with its double-edged axe.

Like the whirling of balls of fluff and music on a cotton piano. Whispering and shuffling, moving and covering. Tubing disconnected, clothing removed, before the stiffness makes it more difficult. Like a shadow play, this whole thousand-headed hospital which is slowly sinking into the darkness of a new day, while a ray of light is laughing in the window and a child talks and talks about life.

The Child's Garden

She is sitting in the shade of the jasmine bush. Its shoots stretch up to the summer sky, but don't bear flowers. Beneath them, the last creamy white blossoms incessantly, or at intervals so short that human noses are unaware of them, send out their sweet scent, faintly enriched with iodine.

Did she cry?

She stretches her legs out over the grass. They give shade to insects and ants that wonder about the mighty bridge that has been built over their customary routes. The hairs on her legs shine red. Will the baby be a redhead as well?

In the linden tree there is a humming afternoon concert. The mallows herald the dusk, their rose color so cool that it is almost gray. She starts. Does someone need food? But it is only the titmouse young, housed, as usual, in the hole where the old telephone cable used to be.

She relaxes again. Bends her legs. Feels a slight weakness in her middle. A lull. No one to carry. No one who sucks. But just now, wasn't that...? No, only the telephone ringing at the neighbor's across the way. The hair on her body curls in the heat. She scratches a mosquito bite. Her nails make a loud scraping noise. It is so quiet all around her. But all at once, a car comes sweeping down from the north and drowns out bird twitter, scraping sound, humming evening concert and the whispering of the wind in the leaves. And now...wasn't that...? Silence.

She stretches and feels how the smallest of her muscles and bones stretch and move. As soon as the little one had struggled out of her, it had started. The echoes, the reflexes, her childhood resurrected. She had fallen asleep curled up like a fetus. Had felt the caress of the cool sheet against the soles of her feet. And now the voluptuous strong backward curving of her spine. She had seen the child, exertion had colored her face dark red, except the muscles and the creases which were pale. Then suddenly, it had smoothed out again like a fan changing its picture because of the whim of an unknown hand.

She sees a star of dampness spread on the blouse-covered hill of her left breast. It is time. Time for a feeding. But all is quiet. Holding the unread book firmly in her left hand, she reaches out with her right to make the carriage glide very slowly towards the lawn and into the shade of the jasmine bush. Then, back again, towards sunshine and her own body smell, which describes an invisible circle around woman, deck chair, baby carriage and jasmine bush.

Yes, there it is now. Very clearly. She jumps up. Unaware of her movements, she jumps and runs. All of it is dictated by an unbridled sense of purpose which ignores fatigue, stiffness, others' looks, backaches and grace. Then she stops suddenly, as when a film is stopped to become a still: the child she heard crying from the house is right here, in the carriage.

She sinks down into her chair. Smiles and looks into her book. The O's make her smile even more, they look so much like the mouth of that person who hungrily forms her lips to make impatient sucking noises. She smiles even more at the association, and lets her eyes wander over the lawn, the dahlia bed, and through the palisade of ash trees towards the road that disappears forever in the green labyrinth of the road map. He who comes walking towards her there one afternoon pushes his blue shadow before him like a wheelbarrow loaded with happiness.

She looks at the juniper shoots, soft-topped ten-year-olds who always lower their heads in an unnoticeable west wind. They remind her of the child. She leans forward and pushes the mosquito netting aside: sleep, pale as marble, breathing so still that she has to feel for it with her cheek. The child radiates warmth, an invisible fur against the unpredictable air that changes every hour.

Covered with hair. A four-chambered heart. Now with bathroom. Kitchen. Mammals. Time for feeding. For suckling. In the past. In the present.

Suddenly the earth split and secreted a moon, they said. It emerged from the slit that is now the Atlantic ditch. It hurled itself into space and remained hairless. It reflects the sun on its shiny billiard-ball surface.

The baby carriage is squeaking in the cherry orchard. Who stole my child? But it's only the song of the yellow warbler.

She grasps the edge of the carriage. Opens the book once more and reads two pages. Engrossed in the text, she suddenly wonders what her hand is holding on to. The edge of a dark box, lined with cloth. There is a weight inside. A rocking weight. What was there before? The feathery lightness of apple blossoms. Then the fruit, hard projectiles. A worm is noiselessly eating its way through the green fruit dangling over her head. And she has a child.

The flag rope is hitting the pole and predicts windy weather. A little mouse is rustling in the leaves next to the stone wall. In the slums of New York, in so many slums, the rats climb up into the beds of children and bite them. Sometimes the children die. Babies chewed on like cheeses. If they even have beds to sleep in.

She has to get up to move the mosquito netting aside. She picks at something black, millimeter-sized on the damp soft cheek. It won't come off. She spits on her finger and removes it. The child tosses in her sleep. Turns her head to the other side. Her eyelids flutter. She sighs deeply, but instead of coming up to the surface sinks back into deep sleep.

She unbuttons her blouse, lets the sun dry the trickle of milk. Food for one who is too little to have anything more than needs. She hears a melancholy whistling from the pines and pictures the bullfinch's Christmas-red breast in the hot summer darkness of the woods. The variously colored ends of the different seasons are tied together like rags in rugs.

Then she swings awhile on a trapeze of dates: born 1970, born 1930, born 1933. Dates are magic. And a lasso for the future. Will the oxygen suffice? In a school in Tokyo the children have headaches and nausea;

rabbits and flowers are already dead. Then, the hot breath of the present embraces her like a pair of arms, she caresses the trunk of the apple tree tenderly and feels the soft roughness of the bark, warm as bread.

Now there is whimpering from the passenger in the carriage. She pushes her back and forth as far as her arm will reach. She feels the rocking of generations of cradles in the muscles of her arm. But the noise grows to a hurricane of hunger. She puts the baby to her breast. Her free hand protects the soft head, sun-warm coconut, like a parasol.

The sucking reaches farther than the roots where the milk wells. She sees the pattern of the rowanberry leaves against the blue, the carnation-red seal on the minutes from the Home and Garden Association's last meeting. Everything becomes distinct and hot, as when contours are branded. There is a happy tiredness that gropes around the bottom of her abdomen with lively crab claws. She contracts like a puppet and the small puppeteer smiles her dolphin smile, quick as the laughter of a sun ray reflected by a moving mirror.

Then she wanders aimlessly through the grass that comes up between her toes. The ash trees are as black now as their flowers. The sun is putting on a shadow play and its reflection in the neighbor's window could be the first evening lamp on the plain.

She hears whimpering and rushes to the carriage. It is empty. She turns around and looks accusingly at the swallow who is playing darts with itself and hits the bull's-eye every time.

The child is asleep in the indoor warmth of the upstairs.

A couple of earwigs have taken possession of the

cold damp baby-carriage bottom. Bats aim at her white blouse. Every car that slows down and then drives by makes her think of the car that will stop. She sees the yellow panes of the gable window. Their reflection in the grass is larger than they are. When she runs up the stairs barefoot she can feel the resilience of the boards responding to the bones of her feet and she feels the soil beneath the house, all the muddy Upland soil spreading in layers and veins, swelling and winding around the earth. And she is in the middle of it all. A point of no return.

Only the angel on the bookmark hovers in the air unconcerned, supported by his billowing wings. Her legs now seem weighed down by the mud, as though she were half buried. Deeply rooted already in the fertile soil of dreams, she is startled by the beginning of a cry. A tyrant reigns over body and rest. Its mouth pouts, its eyes waver. Dead tired, they come together, skin against skin, then a smile flares up and solders them.

She falls asleep with her arm heavy over the child. The distance between them is correct. No dangerous cushions. She thinks about old-fashioned cradles. Breathing as fine as that of an insect veins the silence. Behind the wood panels you can hear the scratching of bat children. She starts. No, someone else has to feed them.

II

She hangs the clothes very close together. The plastic clothesline is stiff and slippery from cold and dew. The sun has just gone down. The clothes will be just as wet and clean tomorrow morning. There will be no bits of leaves or seeds sticking to the cloth; spring is too young to leave traces. The countryside lies clean-shaven after the sharp edges of finally melted crusts of snow. But there is a veil of dampness that will remain intact like the glass of a hothouse, between the sun and the earth.

Her socks are far from his. She moves them closer and smiles at her childishness. The cold should make her hurry. But she takes her time. Feels as though she is picking it up with her fingers, as firmly as she picks up the clothespins. Time belongs to them for a while. And they make use of it together, like two children sucking through straws out of the same glass.

The child's clothes are ridiculous miniatures. That she herself was that size once is indeed a fact, but it is totally incomprehensible. Once we were 78 centimeters tall, and before that 50, 40, 10, 0... A countdown to infinity. Suddenly many incredible things become certain, many absurdities understandable. One should think more about one's previous life, she decides, as she feels the wash water from the clothes run down her arms inside the windbreaker...

She stands still and listens. The house has extinguished its red color, and is brooding, heavy with the approaching night, like a big rock in clear water. The child is sleeping. The starling has left the neighbor's antenna. And the winter-gray squirrel who has hidden his snout under the root of his tail feels the security of his own body warmth and forgets the mite pinching his skin.

The socks of a nine-month-old require two clothespins, just like the socks of a thirty-seven-year-old man. Pleasure puckers the corners of her mouth like lemon juice.

THE CHILD'S GARDEN

The last remaining light is strained through the window panes. It flows slowly from the day; and the emptiness it leaves tries to fill itself with starlight, but only manages specks and sprinkles. The moon is hiding behind the birch. It was there on the lawn near the gate that they had lain cuddled up like cats and warmed its roots during the warmest days of July last year. Still, the birch is just as late as all the other trees. But the cherry is trying to get its bearings with its pointed buds at the end of leaf-green probes that swing up and down in the evening breeze. In the dim light of the porch lamp the boughs seem bent and broken at the joints and they describe half-circles in every direction.

A short while ago snake and lizard, mouse and beetle, rustled in last year's leaves. But now the cold has buried everything with its numbness. In that silence, spring is deliberating whether to come or to go. It is caught in the trap of the seasons just as much as all else is.

In the house silence whispers a few moments, there is pipe smoke and some hurried conversation before the television takes over and she settles down to work upstairs. The whitewood of the new part of the house shines, the new-cut pine surfaces, which will creak and crack and oxidize to yellow. In the glass veranda of the staircase she feels like someone on watch in the top of a lighthouse. She can see in all directions. Listens towards the inside, the nursery. The umbilical cord of the child's crying is not severed, the least little sound pulls at her nerve strings. It will take a while before the two of them are weaned.

She starts working and enjoys the fact that the child

is sleeping. Still, she yields to the temptation to go in and look at her, and in the doorway meets the child's father who has the same intention, to stand there a while and listen to her sleep in the warm, body-scented darkness.

Suddenly she hears heavy steps in the gravel outside. But why hasn't she heard the gate? She jumps up and opens the window. All is quiet. It is someone who wanted her to see the paling of the last streak of light in the western sky. Or who wanted to remind her that the snipe's evening performance is taking place: all around, the air is vibrating with the strange music of his wings. She thinks of a thin membrane, while the sound comes and goes and reminds her of when she played on a comb wrapped in tissue paper. The melody goes on and on, until a soundless plough of wild geese catches her attention and sweeps the soundboard clean. After that all she sees is the swan glimmer in the reeds, whiter than any snow. The cold forces her inside again, into the yellow tent of the lamplight, and the slam of the window wakes the child.

The sobbing comes, reluctant and heavy with sleep. But it doesn't stop. For a long time she hesitates at the door, torn between firmness and spoiling. When she goes in, the child is standing at the foot of the bed, her cheeks wet with tears. She feels the solid warmth of the child's buttocks in her hands as she carries her around to look at paintings and flowers, views and furniture. The child sees well in the dark and names all toys and familiar objects correctly. From time to time a shiver of sobs passes through her and she rubs her forehead sleepily against the big warm body that carries her.

Carefully they walk down the stairs; they creak.

The child laughs at every step, but her laughter is softened by sleepiness, as though she were hesitant about waking herself. The cup next to her mouth is as large as a washbasin, and she sucks in the water greedily. Some of it runs down her chin and joins a trail of tears. Flushed skin becomes visible under the wet nightgown and her eyes are large and heavy with sleep. She carries the muffled soft warmth up the stairs again, then walks slowly through the darkness where the last of the evening light is reflected in the black pier glass with gold decorations and in the glass of the watercolor paintings. She walks and hums softly. Then lowers the baby into the crib very slowly, as though launching a precious vessel. Quickly out of the room on her toes... she stands for a moment in the doorway: yes, the breathing is regular and deep right away.

The whole house relaxes. A sort of peace and serenity spreads in rings from that very small sleep, imprisoned in the cage of the crib. She herself plans to work until midnight, but falls asleep over a book and wakes up two hours later when someone wonders about going to bed sometime soon. Getting undressed she talks about the kite that got caught high up in the birch that morning and had seven knots in its tail. She wonders who had made them.

There is a vase with the first wood anemones on the bedside table. When she picked them two days ago, the wind against her right cheek felt like the wind of death. From the bend of the road she had looked out over the village and thought of those who had died only this past month. What should one do when the wind of death passes over one's cheek?

Weary from having lived through the day, they

abandoned thoughts about such cold winds. The child's breathing rocked them towards a sleepy self-assurance: when morning comes, they will all wake up and be together. Together they will have rowed ahead with double breaths across the waters that separate the living from the unborn. Tomorrow the three of them will be happy together. They should be, but no one can promise it for sure.

When she, half asleep, bent her legs towards her body, she remembered the short bed she had when she was seven, and the cool sheets. When playing hookey was a wonderful night of fever in the middle of the day. What she wanted to do now was to get up despite her tiredness and look at the child for a moment. She knew what she would see. The face would be without contours and it would be shimmering white in the darkness, like a fetus. If she carefully touched the hand that looked as though it had grown out of the sheet, it would perhaps close around her finger.

But she doesn't go to the child's room tonight. Instead she stops at the window to listen to something unknown that is fighting for its life, invisible under the spruce's long skirts. The chase goes back and forth with swishing wings, and death-fearing cries that are thin and frail and come from a very little feather-covered throat.

When finally all is still again, she thinks that the moon is flickering. But it is only the irregularities in the old windowpane that make the light blink as though on a rough sea.

III

The June sky bordered by a rigid round horizon looks as though painted on sheet metal. There is a dove-blue haze that cannot hide the living heat that burns and pierces there like a glowing red-hot needle. Last year's pine needles are drying up and spreading turpentine-like vapors. The trees' chapped bark is peeling off in paper-thin flakes of skin, as though they had sunned too much. The reindeer lichen crumbles under one's feet, it is so dry. Far beneath the cobblestone top of the naked ridge begins the horizon of forests—far away, and softly billowing.

They are sitting in the sun's focal point. Behind their closed eyelids it dances red. From time to time it changes and blinks blue. Then she opens her eyes and puts out her hand. It reaches as far as the child's ankle which feels damp and resilient. A bank of white clouds is drifting steadily north over the forest in the east.

Inside that hot circle of sun the three of them sit very still. The hours have stopped ticking. Even the birds are sluggish in the heat. The very light makes no sound but is felt with all the senses: it filters down to them and merges with the aromas of earth and pine. They are sitting in a crossfire of rising scents, and sweat runs down their bodies. Completely immobile, they inhale the hottest day of the month of June, there on the highest and warmest spot around.

It is the flowers that drew them up here. The child had leaned down from his shoulders and steered them. She had put out her arms and shouted like a monkey. Want flowers, want flowers, want flowers, white flowers, yellow flowers.

They had squatted next to that surprising explosion of floral beauty in the midst of the bone-dry moss. They had carefully touched the shimmering white petals with their finger tips. First they had shouted just like the child: "Look here! And here!" Then the flowers had become too many, they had slowed down and enjoyed them in silence. Only the child had continued tirelessly to shout out her admiration and wonder.

Now the heat has them in its grip, touches them with hot fingers. Their hair gets in their eyes and their foreheads shimmer pale and moist, like the flower petals before.

The child looks around. Sometimes on her knees, sometimes on her bottom. Carefully pats a round-topped rock on the head. Looks up to check whether she is being observed, and then continues with her work.

A dragonfly interrupts the calm with its rustling motor. Its long body swings precariously as though it could break off. When it disappears behind the faded juniper curtains, the heat and silence press down on them like a deep sleep.

She wakes and sees the child ten meters away, poking in the moss, examining, and making a whole series of sounds of study and discovery. The man whom she had thought asleep is watching the child's every movement, his cheek supported on his wrist. A short while ago, he had run fast like a deer through the thicket, rustling leaves and breaking twigs, on his way to the car after something they had forgotten. Then he had dropped onto the heather and moss, breathing hard, his eyes on the child like spotlights.

She sees the clouds moving on and on. An almost unnoticeable change in the quality of the light tells her that the sun is going down. A truck groans under its cargo of lumber on the steep highway below the ridge. A thousand years ago, the highway was here, just here where the rocks are without their lichen skin and mossy fur. The sea stormed, down where the fields now are, and the pastures.

All is still. She looks at the sky. It seems painted on sheet metal. The faraway forests are like waves in a sea, their crests motionless and solidified. Clouds like obedient sheep on their way to the pastures of the northern sky. She feels the moment pierced and held in place by the barbs of her happiness. If the child, only once, once in the life that is still like a tight spring wound up inside her, ready to extend body and soul to something greater and more momentous—if it only once could experience a moment such as this.

He puts cups and a bag of cookies on a flat stone in front of them. There's juice for the child. Everyday sounds from porcelain and spoons. They look at each other with eyes that have been emptied of much that is unnecessary.

The swallows fly back and forth like arrows, as though they were sheep dogs herding the flock of cloud sheep. But she doesn't say this to the child. To see the clouds and swallows is wonderful enough.

IV

It rained all through the night. At dawn the drops were sparse and sounded like the blows of a hammer. The morning light fell more obliquely, and when the sun came out it had a darker shine.

She walked slowly on grass that was limp from the rain. Where the child's pool had been, the vegetation was flat and brown. They had moved it now so as to avoid a permanent scarring of the lawn. She felt the water; it had cooled during the night. The sun was still behind the birch and was taking its time about raising the temperature. On the plastic bottom of the pool there was a thin layer of something slippery: dissolved pollen, leaves of grass that had followed the child's feet into the water, jasmine blossoms, now of a thinner whiteness from the night rain and the water in the pool. It was easy to fish up a ladybug with your hand and throw it out together with the water that had almost drowned it.

A red-striped beetle was floating farther away, between a blue ball and a yellow plastic duck. Its feelers were moving and you could hear a sharp buzzing sound from its struggle with death. A death in miniature, but just as absolute as the eradication of a city or a forest. The hair-fine boundary between movement and immobility, acting and being acted upon. She kneeled at the edge of the pool and cupped her hand under the long sturdy insect. Almost three centimeters long, she reflected, planning to look it up. The brick-red stripes went across the wings, and the feelers that were moving slowly and laboriously were of the same color.

Then she saw that the animal was a raft invaded by pirates. They were working frenetically around the front edge of its carapace. They swarmed from the edges of the wings towards the bug's underside. They fumbled with their spidery legs around the feelers as though to immobilize them. At first they seemed small and helpless against the very bulk of the insect. But when she touched one of them with a blade of grass, she understood that they already were the victors: it didn't move, was stuck as if by suction and some poisonous substance and seemed engrossed in its destructive work as though in great pleasure.

They were a hundred against one. They were in power. But the big bug was still alive. What she was holding in her hand was a courtroom in which all of the neatly khaki-dressed judges had long ago agreed upon capital punishment, and the criminal, sweaty and smelling of urine because of his dread, was a living cadaver in his striped costume, an apparition from another world; but he could still wave lamely with his arms. No one wanted to touch them even though they were so strangely alive.

She put the insect and its silent executioners on the grass. Then remembered the child's quick fingers, all-seeing eyes under the frowning eyebrows. In some obscure way she wanted to keep her from the knowledge of what was most grim. And although she knew that it was a futile gesture, she moved the beetle that was slowly being devoured and buzzing through its dread to a wild-rose leaf.

When she turned her back, the whole disorderly cluster fell to the ground. Some of the khaki-dressed judges got caught in a spider web, where dew drops five times their size met them with the enormous strength of surface tension, like spheres made of lead.

She looked toward the house and listened. Saw the old boards worn by many years of rain, their color paled to different shades of red. A veil of white hung down from the window ledges, as though something were being aired even though the windows were closed. During the storm last July, when the pine ridge acquired new fire breaks, and an old brickworks was torn down without cost to the owner, the red house paint was pressed through the cracks in the windows. There was still a little pile of red powder inside each window frame. In this way, the indoors and the outdoors tried to blend; it was a period of osmosis caused by the pressure of wind and wetness. Much was now happening during the August heat, a process of transformation, of fermentation, which would not stop until it was cooled and calmed by the hand of winter.

As though in a dream, she walked towards the colorful clothes on the line. She brushed away the earwigs and then took down cotton jumpers that had become stiff from drying in the sun. She rubbed them soft and breathed in the smell of clean cloth. She stood immobile in a hollow of silence. The voices of the birds took longer and longer pauses. The crickets' instruments were so delicate that you couldn't hear them up here in the woods. Behind the mosquito netting of the nursery someone moved around and kicked the bars of the crib with muffled thuds. She yearned to see a hand draw aside the curtain and to hear the child speak clearly, but at the same time she wanted to hold on to this moment. And then the call drew her like a puppet up the stairs and through the room to reach the helpless dictator.

That night the thunderstorm came. It ripped and pounded. It roared and flashed with its police searchlights. No one was exempted. No one was spared.

The adults pulled out electric plugs, closed windows. Then they talked as usual. But mostly about fear of thunderstorms.

When they got upstairs, they found her standing in her crib, crying. The last of the crashes had waked her up. And awake, she had seen how the light in the room was turned on and off as though by a hysterical hand. The whole garden was flickering: sometimes blue-white, sometimes in the clearest shades of daylight. The sealing-wax red of the carnations lit up and was gone. The pink clusters of phlox appeared and disappeared again. The sweeping bottom branches of the spruce bowed in derision and then retired into darkness. The world was involved in a scary game of peekaboo, and it was very obvious that the songs and laughter of the grownups had no connection with the game going on outside. Theirs was pitiful prattle: they were children being used for playing games.

The candlelight, warm drinks, soft accordion music and comfort of her daddy's arms soon made her laugh. Only when the thunder was so close that crash and light came simultaneously did she hide her face.

Memories flew through the room, clothed in words or silent and naked. They dealt with thunderstorms in the archipelago, thunder in a rowboat on Lake Tullinge, just when the perches were biting, tropical storms when the car had filled with water and the bilharzia larvae were an invisible but worried-about threat too momentous to forget.

Only let there be no bombs... let there be no bombs. Not now. Not in the future. In the child's future. They looked at each other, the man and the woman, and the child was sleeping against his breast. If there really are prayers, then this was one, and the strongest of them all.

V

Whenever they woke at night, they could hear the flagpole whipping itself with its rope. A flagellant, white and slender, on exhibit in the middle of the meadow.

The wind went on and on and didn't seem ever to arrive at its destination. A wicker chair soaked up the humidity and creaked, stretching its knotty limbs. An invisible being walked across the living-room floor. She remembered the mouse she had chased out with the broom: how it had thrown itself down and twisted its body on the stairs and exposed its pale stomach. From the child's room they heard the sound of a vigorous kick. She could reach the bars of the crib now, and they would have to worry about their sturdiness. She herself felt an echo of those kicks against her insides. The child got ready and set and dived into another dream.

The curtain breathed in and out. Sometimes it was outside as though waving from a train compartment. Sometimes it bulged inward like a sail that wanted to get the whole room on the move. A fox got excited far off in the valley: its sound reached their ears like a trail of swaying waves. Then the child kicked again and whimpered. They waited with bated breath: would she fall asleep again, or did she need help?

One single green lacewing had survived in the artificial summer of the room. It was tapping dryly against the ceiling. It had been driven upward by the current of warm air. Its relatives lay dead between the flower pots in the next room. The green in their thin long wings had faded like leaves in the fall. Their eyes, metallic like those of marzipan pigs, were covered by a layer of death, and no longer shiny.

Once they had awakened and thought that the house was on fire. They could hear it crackling and spitting. It had already reached the attic! But instead it was hundreds of green lacewings that had found their way in and were dancing unrhythmically against the ceiling. As a child she had loved green lacewings more than any other insect. She had called them golden princesses because of their eyes, despite the fact that she knew very well that they were called "stinkwings." But she had never smelled anything. She had only seen in them a delicate beauty, which she had asked her grandmother to copy for a costume: green lampshade tulle with a golden belt.

That night, when they realized that the crackling of the fire was an invasion of green lacewings, her feelings for them changed. There were too many. Carefully, they fanned them out through the window. But before the mosquito netting was fastened the insects slipped in again. After a while they fell asleep to the sound of the world's smallest castanets.

The refrigerator began to hum. "Sh!" she said, "Don't wake the child!"

But technology continued inexorably with its secret processes. The heating system chimed in and sang and snapped. When the cold from the outside met the inside warmth, the radiator contracted with a bang, like a baking sheet that is cooling.

The child's whimpering became louder. It made the night a few shades lighter. Waking life leaked in.

He reached over to light the lamp.

Just then, a large truck started to make its way up

from the village. They could hear it already from several kilometers' distance. At first the sound was as low as that of a mosquito. Easy to mistake for an illusion. But the illusion came closer and grew to the uneven thump and drone of a fly. Then it sounded like a car, or a truck further away to the north on its way through the woods, where it can drive for miles without seeing yellow window squares making holes in the darkness.

Now there was no doubt about it. A twelve- or sixteen-wheel mastodon of a trailer-truck was bulling up the road, its headlights like snowplows. Darkness fled. Silence as well.

The child was quiet. Was listening to the noise of the motor coming closer. Her eyes moved under thin-skinned blue-veined lids. One could see these movements if one watched closely. Like arms and legs moving under a blanket.

The house stood tense and listened. The floors stopped squeaking. The refrigerator had completed its electric cycle and was freezing the food silently. The wicker chair had stopped creaking. Or was it the loudness of the motor that had drowned out all of these lesser noises? You could certainly not hear the surviving green lacewing tapping against the ceiling.

Now the child started to cry. But softly, half asleep. "Oh," she complained, "we need some sleep!"

The truck grumbled on like continuous thunder. It was still beyond the store. Soon there would no longer be any barrier for its noise.

The child whimpered plaintively. Howled from time to time and strained their nerves. They hardened themselves and didn't move. Maybe she'd fall asleep again.

Now came the curve and then the truck accelerated. The noise drowned out the child's crying. The truck roared by. Its noise trailed behind. In cottage after cottage people woke and turned over.
But in the nursery all was quiet.
Sinking into sleep, they mumbled:
"The truck took away her crying!"
"It's on its way through the country now to collect children's miseries and nightmares."
"That's why it had so many trailers."
"In the cab someone sits and hums a tune, his face illuminated from below by the dashboard lights, so that he looks like an Indian god."
"The god of good sleep is on his way to the north."
"And he sweeps up all the sobbing and whimpering, howling and sadness, and doesn't dump it until he reaches the sea..."
"That should help raise the water level of the Baltic."
"Sh! Don't wake her."
The drone of the motor was dying now. A diminuendo that was so gradual that no one could say when it died. But you could again hear the green lacewing. And the first rooster; then little cars started their fussy swishing, swish, swoosh, they swept the road. And the earth slowly turned the other cheek.

Left Alone

IN THE EVENING she crept down between the sheets and thought about death. She'd always done that, even during happy times. Sister would then call from the blue room:

"Are you sleeping yet?"

And she'd answer:

"Not yet, my dear, I'm lying here thinking."

Now all was silent in the room. There was silence everywhere. She longed for the fall rain to drum on the roof, or for a storm that would chase her out of bed to lock the front door—it had the annoying habit of opening with the slightest draft. How often had they not discussed getting it repaired?

"It has to be sawed up and then straightened," the foreman at the carpenter's had said.

"Won't it be very ugly then?" Sister had asked.

"Guess you can cover it up with putty," said the foreman's son who was hanging around, poking in his ears with a match.

At that they had become doubtful and decided that

the door was old and beautiful, and that they could very well push it shut a little longer, another winter. They would decide then.

What they would do then, they hadn't thought about any further. They had walked through the park, away from the highway, and swung their arms; that's good exercise, Sister had said. But Ella's arms were so short that she had felt silly flapping them around like a penguin.

Now she placed those arms on her blanket and saw how the moonlight fell on them. They are getting just like grandmother's, she was thinking, full of brown spots and furrowed like newly plowed fields.

"Sister?" she said in a half-whisper. But no one answered. The brown walnut bed was undisturbed. The crocheted spread was no longer removed for the night.

The suburbs of the city surrounded their hill. Nights were not as dark as during their childhood. The silence not as silent.

"How dreadful will it be?" she was wondering. She had a daughter in town who was working at a hospital, and the things she talked about were terrible. No matter how much one tried to get used to the idea, one always was surprised, and died with a stupid expression on one's face, she was thinking. And actually, it wasn't anything you had to get used to, since you only went through it once. Once and never again. After that it is over. Everything. All over.

But when Sister died she'd run into the woods behind the house. She would never be able to admit that to a living soul—thank God there was no longer any obligatory confession, no one was religious any more. I went down to the kitchen and warmed some water for her tea with honey, she had said, and when I came upstairs she was gone.

"What do you mean, gone?" her daughter had asked on the telephone, for even though she was crying and distressed about her old aunt, she wanted to know exactly what had happened.

"She was dead," Ella had said. "She was staring right up into the air, and her neck seemed all tense. I closed her eyelids and tried to make her lie down flat on the bed. It was so strange, but what I was thinking just then was that she should be lying nicely, you see? It felt awful, as though I were some sort of hostess who was about to invite people to look at her. And even then I forgot her hands, so they stiffened the way she had had them at that point, that last moment."

But the fact was that she had run straight out into the woods crying, that she couldn't tell anyone. And that she had left her sister alone in her agony with that cold hand extended and with words that could mean anything at all but which, behind the slurring and the dry cracked lips, must have meant: I don't want to. It was something she would never be able to talk about, something she would have to carry all alone until her own memory was extinguished, and she would be carried away like a thing.

A little bit of flesh and bones, she was thinking. A thing without a soul. And she remembered the fly that had buzzed and buzzed so infernally in the kitchen until she lost patience and hit it with the local newspaper. After that it had been nothing more than a fluff of legs and wings that she could blow out of the window into the fall grass, to become a bit of fertilizer in the soil. What is it that had happened there, there on that razor-fine edge between buzz and silence, between struggle and immobility? She could brood over that until the sun came up on the horizon behind the high-rises.

Now the moon was shining on the wallpaper, discoloring its pale roses and bleaching their leaves. What was colorful during the day was now black and white. Nuances disappeared and the same happened to thoughts at night, she decided. They too became black and white, hard and unreconciled. Daytime and sunlight mellowed them. I am not alone under the ban, she was thinking, we are all equal before death, but that doesn't make me hate it less.

The sheets rustled as she turned in her bed. She looked around the room. On the round table there were newspapers from several days, untidily folded around their obituaries and their guerrilla wars. No, not theirs, she corrected herself. It was reality. The screw of the garrote and the bullet in the heart, dropping to the ground, the mouthful of sea water. Reality. Just like Sister who is dead. We had talked about it so often:

"Which one of us?"

"I hope both of us at the same time!" They had laughed and hugged each other. At other times they had been worried:

"What will happen to you?"

"And what about you, my dear? Together we are strong. But the strength will remain with the one who is left, don't you think?"

Which one of them had said that? She tried to remember now, as though there were an omen in those words. But she couldn't hear the voice behind them. In the dark of the night they were as though embroidered with moon thread on the blue window shade. The strength will remain... But what's the use, she was thinking, and had to admit that it was a meaningless thought. A vague and pointless thought. Meaning and use. One had to live without them. They were outgrown children's shoes, that weren't worth gilding and putting on the bookshelf.

When they had thought about such things, Sister and she, they had lit a candle and taken out a bottle of bourgogne. They had made a fire in the fireplace, even in the middle of summer, and then read Dostoevsky aloud to each other, and household chores had had to wait. They had tried to go into a room that was their special common home, as Sister had called it, where they could warm themselves, and where Goethe had walked and Kant pondered, where Dickens had told tales, and Nijinsky had leapt. The common home was the little house human beings helped each other to create to protect themselves from the icy winds of the inexplicable and the black holes of meaninglessness. It's a good thing we have learned to read, they had said, and had gone to the library the next day to get a new load of learning.

Now it will be the room where she had been left alone, Ella was thinking, although the others are still here, so it is wrong to think this way. But what if I play hooky? If I start living mechanically, darting back and forth between the supermarket and the meeting of the housewives' association, between filling in as a substitute at the druggist's and the more and more frequent dull, dreary hours watching television?

Better be completely dead than like a wound-up machine, merely playing a human role and pretending a human smile, while already half-dead and more a thing than a human being. Those are the sort of people who can hurt you in a crowd: they don't push with their elbows, they jab like table corners and cut like knives.

Then she heard the hoot of an owl. It split the night. And in a lull between the roar of trucks, from far away across many kilometers of roofs shining in the moonlight, the answer came softly.

She lay there listening to the eager loving pair as they dominated the great outdoors on the outskirts of the city. They filled space from boulder-ridge to railroad, from sand pit to the edge of the lake with their noisy duet. They didn't have secrets. On the contrary, they exulted in their belief that they were the only ones awake, and they imagined they were the only lovers. They ignored all else: bus traffic, a weather-bureau plane, an ambulance siren, a motorcycle without muffler. All that they shooed away. Here there's only us, the winners in a countrywide contest for the best popular love song.

She'd always liked owls and other birds of prey. Sister had decided that she had Indian blood in her veins and that she was honoring an ancient totem when she stood stock-still watching for a wide-winged sailor in the sky. No one could hear the approach of a buzzard as well as she, and she'd drop everything to run out to the courtyard:

"Sis! Sis! Do you hear the buzzard?"

And when they drove along country roads she bent down to look through the windshield and took her hands off the steering wheel to point at something, and the car swayed dangerously, and Sister screamed:

"Hold on to the steering wheel, woman! You're going to kill us for the sake of a miserable hawk!"

"Hawk!" Ella said, injured. "That was an osprey." There they stood that time, panting from the scare, and a man with a trailer was scolding them, honking his horn, and a slow yellow tractor they had just passed overtook them and the driver laughed.

She lay there and thought about ospreys: shining white underneath and with their fringed wings at a sharp angle. She could feel her stomach tighten with delight at seeing the bird sailing there, over the valley, just when she had happened to look up. Would he seem as beautiful now, when she no longer had anyone to show him to?

Towards morning the wind started blowing. She woke to a full storm. The birches were sweeping the ground and the pines got rid of their dry branches and the last of the apples thudded to the earth, so she had to stoop on her way to the mailbox.

She stood at the gate for a long time, resting her elbows on it. The bank manager drove by and rolled down his window to say that the sheep pasture was full of mushrooms. The old druggist rode by on his bicycle, almost dragging his German shepherd. They greeted each other, but he didn't dare get off, it seemed, because they were in such good balance just then, he, the bicycle and the dog. The neighbor's Emma sauntered by with her bright yellow plastic schoolbag, and then stopped at the corner to wait for the school bus.

I could take a kitchen chair and sit in the middle of the intersection and become an eccentric, she was thinking. And the day would go by with all the people who'd talk to me, or just ask me to move a little so that they could get past with their different vehicles.

There was a picture postcard from her daughter and her boyfriend who were at a political conference in Roskilde. There was a letter from her lifelong friend and colleague who now had Parkinson's disease and was slowly languishing away in Västervik. There was a thick catalogue with all the new fashions for the fall, and also the Stockholm *Daily News*, and the local newspaper.

But instead of going in with the mail, she dropped it on the porch. The wind started to leaf through the bright clothes for boys and girls, middle-aged and old women. It undressed and dressed them again and treated them as though they were wilted leaves.

The wind blew from behind her and she felt as though there were a vacuum around her which made her breathe twice as deeply. Then she climbed to the top of the hill with the birches, as far as the boulder where her sister had had her herb garden. It was only two months since she had died, but the patch already looked abandoned. The tarragon should have been picked long ago, and late-summer grass had grown over the hyssop. The chervil was white with mildew and a hop vine had been torn loose by the storm and was waving helplessly with its pale green cones.

I shall, I shall, she mumbled and climbed through the wild raspberry bushes to the top of the hill. This was where the summer pavilion had been. Eight-cornered with built-in benches and beautiful soft-colored paintings on the ceiling. In the middle of the floor there had been a drop-leaf table, and against one of the walls a little stove. But the roof had decayed and collapsed and, with the assistance of the City Museum, they had carefully dismantled it and had stored what was left in the old woodshed. They had planned to restore it. They should have begun just at this time, and Sister had said very recently:

"We're going to sit there when the fall winds howl and roast apples and read old poetry."

Ella walked there now and sobbed with anger.

"Why did you say that when you didn't mean it? When you just went away like that and left me in the lurch!"

She was surprised that she really felt angry, wronged by death. That's the healing process, she was thinking, sorrow's self-healing process. It is the way to become strong and healthy again, as the doctor said. Healthy for whom? Strong for what?

She walked straight through the pavilion and saw its colored windowpanes shining in the sunshine. What if I should rebuild it in Sister's memory! I shall drive to the museum and look at photographs in the archives. I can do the drawings on the dining-room table, and talk with that excellent carpenter in Björklinge.

Then she stumbled over a bough and looked up. The tallest of the aspen had lost an arm. The bough was thick and healthy and about as long as a full-grown human being. It just lay there in the grass, simply torn off. She stood there for a long time looking at it. What was it that was so remarkable about a torn-off aspen bough? Then she saw it: the wind played with its leaves just as though they were still alive. And the leaves trembled and whisked in the stiff September breeze and behaved as though they didn't have the slightest idea that they were already doomed.

The Nothingness Forest

First there was laughter and play. The lamp that dazzled. And she screwed up her eyes. Her toes struggled inside the warm hand. But she didn't remember that now.

The smell and the smoothness of the ointment. Someone who carefully touches her skin where it's most sensitive. The voice that blows well-known breath into her nostrils. The delicate cleanliness of the paper diaper. The rustling of plastic. Tight clothes that are forced over one's head and entangle one's legs. Someone puts her on a stool and her feet don't reach the floor.

She thinks she's flying, and is dizzy with glee. Then she hits the ground and her laughter turns to crying without one second's hesitation.

She stops crying and listens. No answer. She cries harder. But the only thing she hears is the echo of a closing door. And the silence becomes deeper.

The silence is so deep that it makes her silent too. Smothered and scared by the silence, she crawls and slides across the floor, bumps her forehead and comes to a stop on her hands and knees, as immobile as a railroad car at the terminal.

Then she hears something scratching and whining. Scratching and whining and enticing. Like laughing. Like feeling a woolly coat of fur.

She gurgles with delight and gets up. She stands unsteadily with the diaper hanging heavy in the back. The door handle moves up and down and the dog comes in.

They hug each other. The four shaggy legs hug the four that are crooked and clothed. The tongue licks warmly and pleasantly. She chokes and struggles. Long before the dog manages to put a stop to the bowing and scraping of his affection, she is interested in something else. Her back straight, she stands determined, with one hand deep in his fur.

Although the dog is several times her size, he feels the human power of that little fist. He succeeds in controlling the waggings and droolings of his bliss, and he, too, looks forward with determination. Now they see the gate.

Two pairs of eyes at an equal level above the ground see a gate. It cuts freedom and air and greenery into thin strips. The handle rests like a punctuation dash for reflection, horizontally in the air. But reflection is not their specialty. And without a thought, without a stumble, without delay, they reach the gate.

The dog, having practiced on many handles, manages the gate handle easily. Now there is the crunch of gravel under their paws and soles. They're on their way!

* * *

On that day a high-pressure system over central Sweden has decided to move southward. It does so slowly and reluctantly. It has lain comfortably over the swaybacked meadows of Upland, and it has clung to the rugged branches of the juniper pine covered hillsides. It has filtered through the newly unfolded birch foliage, and sniffed along fields of wood anemones, bitter vetch, and the just-formed little leaves that can become anything when summer comes.

The winds of departure come in gusts. They give and they take. There's an excitement in the air. Do they feel it, perhaps, the dog and the child, as they start out?

Behind them in the villa no one suspects anything. It is an uneventful weekday. No one suspects that everything is about to change, just as no one suspects a change in the beautiful spring weather. There are no foreboding signs. Except perhaps the calm, the very silence.

All at once walking is so very easy. The four paws tramp eagerly. The two feet stamp in their cotton socks. Her hand deeply inbedded in the fur: a fistful of security, shaggy and strong.

And so, without stopping, they wander down the street where all the windows seem to look the other way, and they disappear on the path into the forest. A schoolboy on his bicycle turns a corner one second too late. He had had trouble with his shoestrings. The lady who is beating her rugs got dust in her eyes and runs into the house to look in the mirror. As though enveloped in a cloak of invisibility, they enter the realm of the blueberry bushes.

* * *

She starts humming to herself. The dog walks on and listens. His ears bend forward, to the side: What is she saying? Shall I obey? But the sounds aren't really human sounds yet. I won't pay attention to them, he decides. Just then she suddenly says clearly and loudly: "Doggy!"

He jumps with surprise. With his front paws apart, he stands there and wags his tail.

As a result of his sudden reaction, she falls down on her bottom. But gets up right away, and walks on. Alone.

The dog barks.

"Doggy," she repeats stubbornly. And he joins her.

Now she is the leader. She is singing something incomprehensible while beating time with her arms. She laughs when the gusts of wind whisk around her legs, and at the wagtail that's there one minute, gone the next, and then back again. They play at peekaboo like Mommy and Daddy.

"Peekaboo," says the child. And the bird disappears.

The dog has started to run around in circles. Catches the scent of mice and rabbits on the wet reception tip of his muzzle. The chattering of squirrels makes him stand on his hind legs with his eyes riveted upon a pine. Then, down on all fours again, he circles around the child, who as though pulled by a string is advancing straight as an arrow into the forest.

A coast guard helicopter skims the tree tops. Had it not received orders to look for imagined enemies, it would have noticed the geometric figure described by the dog and the child: a circle with a moving radius.

Airplanes and helicopters are nothing new for the

child and the dog. They walk happily in the dark forest. The temperature falls a few degrees. The food in their stomachs settles down. An uncertainty about direction and goal intrudes upon their spirit of adventure. But these signals aren't strong enough to stop them. They continue to quickly move away from the town.

Someone looking at the community from above, with the eyes of an interested giant bending down to see, hands on his knees and with his shoulders at the level of the lowest clouds, would observe a strange commotion, like a whirlwind of people and feelings, of exclaiming and lamenting. Also, cars are crowding around one of the villas. People get out and get back in. Exhaust fumes shine with a bluish hue in the midday sunshine. Someone is crying and cannot be comforted.

But in the dark of the forest there is a smell of resin, and the pine needles glitter. Feet leave no tracks. The scent of violets and pine combines with a pungent odor from the ever heavier contents of the child's plastic pants. She tries to scratch, and the dog sniffs with interest several times. Then she grabs hold of his fur, and they do another kilometer at a slow trot.

A squirrel drops gnawed-off pine cones on the pair. A flock of bullfinches shines like toadstools against golden maidenhair. The silence thickens under the low branches. The lichen retains the warmth of the day and so doesn't heed the signals of change in the weather. The child walks more slowly now and her socks have absorbed moisture from the path.

At that moment someone calls the child's name. It

is a long and mournful call. An enormous voice that seems to swallow them both, that seems to take them into its round mouth and then slowly drop them again onto the path.

They listen in the same direction, the child and the dog. Try to take a few steps towards it. But last year's brown meadowsweet is thick there and a fallen tree blocks their way with its pointed roots. So they continue along the path, slowly and hesitatingly. Soon they forget the call, but its echo makes them uneasy.

There it is again: the child's name. A man's deep voice. Nobody they know. The voice is vehement and urgent. It sounds like an order and the dog looks questioningly at the child. He stands in the child's way, inclines his head and waits for an initiative from this very small human being.

But she looks at him and laughs and says her "Doggy!"

That awakens his sense of duty and he bumps into her so that she has to sit down on the path. When she tries to get up, he bumps her again. The dog is trying to shove her in the direction of the calls, but the child is only aware of his keeping her from the one thing that is important and fun: walking. For the first time in her life she has discovered the trick of walking, and so wants to keep going and going to see how long it can last.

Now the name is blaring through the forest, and the dog is very worried. He stands over the child and gently takes hold of the back of her jumper with his teeth, as though she were a puppy.

That makes the child angry.

"Bad!" she says. "Bad dog!!!"

That makes the dog meek and submissive. But when

the child's name resounds again and again, further away this time, his excitement returns. Something is expected of him, he is sure of that, something is happening, there is a connection between the shouts and the little child who is lying on her back now looking at him with angry eyes, her forehead creased.

"Bad doggy! Go away!"

The dog steps away from the child and thoughtfully lies down on the mossy ground. With his muzzle resting on his front paws, he looks at the cotton-clothed mystery, who, although almost hairless and with crooked legs, has the commanding glint in her eyes which he has learned to obey, always.

He whines and whisks his tail around ingratiatingly. The shouts come from a greater distance now. When he attempts to bark, his conflicting emotions transform the bark into a squeak.

Once again he tries to persuade the child by standing close to her. She has gotten up and is standing unsteadily, looking hard at him. He comes closer and opens his jaws as much as he can: she is a foolish and disobedient puppy who has to be carried home to her basket.

At that, the child's fist lands full force right on his soft upper lip. Behind it is the hard jawbone, so the effect is considerable. The dog howls and retreats.

"Go away! Bad dog!" the child commands and takes a few steps towards him.

Ashamed and confused, dragging his tail, the dog disappears like a shadow. The loud human voices attract him with their promise of more certain commands and soothing pats on the back. Like a shadow he disappears. Then all is quiet.

* * *

The shouts are only a mumble now, and easily drowned by low-flying bumblebees. There is a rumbling in the child's stomach that commands all of her attention. She listens to it. Food. Water. She trots on.

At a bend in the road, she meets loneliness. All at once she realizes without any words: far away, no mommy, no daddy, no lady, no dog. Hungry and lonely.

She cries with a loud and reproachful voice. But the pine seedlings don't pay any attention to her accusations, and the gathering clouds that she can see, now that the forest has thinned, are only gray and uninterested.

Her howling rises and falls. She has to sit down in order to have enough strength to cry as she clenches her fists, and her feet inside the dirty, wet cotton socks. So that's what the world is like. Once upon a time there was a bright light that dazzled, and a warm hand around her feet. She doesn't remember it, but misses it anyway. Because it's not that way now.

Here, the pine needles stick and hunger aches and the low clouds are damp and uncomfortably cold. Here there is loneliness without bounds.

As though the child could see the hopelessness in her situation from the outside, she stops crying. For what good is it to cry at the threshold of horror and the utmost limit of misery?

Quietly she sits there and picks up earth and tender grass. Drops it again. She plucks with her fingers and her hands in the same way as the very old do with the roses on their last blanket, the folds in their sheets. As though she wanted to prepare, gather strength to meet the Horrible.

But the Horrible doesn't come. Only dusk gathering more and more. Only fog that licks her cheeks, and sleep that moves inside of her warm and soft. Mild gray Nothingness is all there is, and it is worse than fear.

The cold rises from the earth. Slowly her eyes turn inward. An erring ant examines the seam of her jumper.

The evening tide wipes away the last remains of day. Outlines are erased. Pines and stones, moss and child, all sink into the fog. She learns that the created can be lifeless, can be a thing, and that the joy of life needs both a striking surface and a match in order to glimmer. She sits there, heavy with hunger and loneliness and turns into a thing.

Therefore, she doesn't move when the man in the windbreaker bends over her with a happy cry and lifts her into his arms. Therefore, she turns away when Mommy's teary face, an eon later, bends down over her.

For many days she avoids meeting their eyes. They are so inexperienced, so young, they know nothing about life. They have not seen, and some of them will never see, the great nothingness she met in the forest.

The Eagle Cage

Dawn brushes the roof with dew. The sun bakes it to a black crust. The walls are gray like yeast. Mortar snows into the rosebushes. The gardener sprays and curses. The mildew is back again next day. Still the roses bloom miraculously.

The inhabitants never walk on grass still wet with dew. The early morning sun is used up when they come out on the steps to squint cautiously towards the curtain of leaves which hides the world. The walks lie well combed before them. One kilometer, then gate and fence. Outside is freedom—freeways, ready for use. They will ride there in an ambulance or coffin.

Often they stand in groups on the staircase and cannot decide whether to go up or down. There is always some meal to wait for, no matter how far off. The fittest of them lives on the third floor and never uses the elevator. He'll brag himself into a heart attack. But until then he holds court on his landing.

They ruffle their feathers in front of the north windows like old eagles. They shrug their shoulders, stroke

their bellies where the Sunday feasting of a whole lifetime has left layers of fat. Their thoughts are as worn as their best suits. Their words are threadbare.
"We're really well off here!"
Or: "She treats us rotten. Did you hear what she said to Lönnbeck today?"
"Well, I couldn't eat that yucky mess."
"When the old king was still alive, we often had dinner at the Continental, my little girl and I..."
The rake wanders fastidiously over the early morning paths: the artificial snoring of the sleepless. Dandruff falls like mildew onto shoulders.
"He cuts miserably, the scoundrel, and charges four crowns for it!"
"What's more, he owns a car..."
"Everybody has a car, nowadays. Not like in the old days when I was young. In those days you learned what work and hardship were like. Real work, and real hardship, that is!"
In the darkest recess of the corridor someone lies in wait to sneer: "Your son's sure not been here for a long time!"
A hunched back shuffles away across the red linoleum.
"I see Bäck isn't condescending to eat with us today..."
The sparrows who live in the hedge paint its thorns elegantly with their droppings which gleam all through the year like white berries. Some of the men feed the birds with crumbs. Others save their leftover bread in trunks and boxes until weevils start crawling down the corridors and knock at the door of the kitchen personnel's living quarters. Then there's thorough house-

cleaning and airing. Next day, they start storing their leftovers all over again. For a rainy day.

One hundred sparrows. Two men. They look after the gate. With cloudy eyes where the white and the blue are gradually blending, they contemplate the dusty cars that sweep by. One or another of them slows down to read the sign, starts up again with frightening speed. Then it's gone.

"Let's go see my old man. No more'n a nice ride really. Regular countryside out there. Back home in no time."

And the young wife finally agrees.

Whose son? Many pairs of eyes wonder. Or whose attorney? Aha! His crazy divorced wife. Now she comes and puts on airs. When he's got one week left. At the most, the doctor said.

The wind blows the smell of camphor through the sick room. It is the only thing that moves. Under the blanket tent the bedsores eat up his back soundlessly. Silence. Suddenly a bouquet of flowers indicates that someone has been there. A head, unnaturally large and near, screams: "Coffee! Coffee!! Coffee!!!"

He no longer wants to understand. The healthiest of them stands in the doorway and shouts: "Hi there! Hi, Charley!"

"I want to die. I just want to die now," someone says on the landing. No one contradicts him. What's the matter with those bastards? Why doesn't somebody say something? Do they think I'm planning to die standing right here and now maybe?

A low-pressure front comes rolling down from the attic. A sweaty maid draws laundry baskets back and forth. The nails under them squeak on the marble floors. Suddenly the foliage is gray and dust from the gravel-covered courtyard irritates people's nostrils. Two men try to get into the elevator at the same time: one wants up to his room, the other down to the bath. They pull and push each other around and hiss like great helpless spiders.

"You bastard! I'll show you...!"

A crutch flashes like lightning. Next minute there is a roll of thunder.

"Gentlemen! Gentlemen!" mumbles one who's forgotten he is deaf, and so no one hears him. Others screech excitedly, like birds of prey. A couple of starched white aprons wave their angel wings and cool the atmosphere. They spread a scent of schoolmarm and lavender soap. Rain splashes onto the gravel and slowly eradicates the lines made by the rake. Soon all that is left in the staircase is the echo of the quarrel.

When the bell rings, they stretch, suspended in the dim light of their daydreams. The sky outside their windows is so blue that they think the shades are drawn. Armchairs squeak. A chewed cigar butt is squashed ceremoniously. The plush bedspread with Persian decoration is smoothed by blue-veined fingers, crooked like claws. Somebody looks for his glasses and mutters, then unexpectedly finds a magnifying glass he'd lost before. A random smile wanders towards the shelf under the mirror, where a grandchild babbles in a silver frame. Slippers shuffle. Someone breathlessly ties the shoestrings of a pair of cracked kid shoes—elegant thirty years ago, and shined both on Times Square and Place de la Concorde.

They fumble with their greetings, have already met fifteen times today. Pushing or bowing, they stream into the dining room. A latecomer limps along the hallway. Some stay in their rooms. Hungry or dead.

For fifteen minutes the clatter of their knives and forks drowns out the chattering of the sparrows.

"There's nothing but junk on TV!"

"Yes, but..."

"Junk! That's all there is."

He's a millionaire and gets the last word. A former game warden raises his coffee cup bending his little finger daintily.

"And what about you, sir, you're an artist. Do you have anything hanging at the National Museum?"

Fading in his room, there are some still-gaudy ribbons of the sort used for wreaths. Death supplied him with a clientele, calligraphy and gilding were his specialties. In his family he had been both black sheep and light-blue hope. But no one is alive to reproach him now.

Rheumatism bends him to look like a living scythe. The very blade stabs him in the neck whenever he tries to straighten his back.

"The then crown princess was my customer!"

"Well, I was friends with a man who had been her, well, her lover..."

"My dear man..."

Clouds of cigar smoke.

"That I heard about before. There isn't a thing I haven't heard about."

"And she behaved just like any other chick. Those were his words. Not mine."

He curls his purplish-blue lips as though the very hours disgusted him. Sensually, he combines snuff with his coffee. A piece of sugar is dissolving under his tongue.

Attached to his glasses there is a little lever that lifts his eyelids. A girl once asked him to get that defect operated on. That was the end of the romance. Secondrate love, he had decided, relieved.

"Have I told you about my daughters? They really are outstanding. Just today..."

"A woman's place is in the kitchen and in bed. That way they're busy day and night. That's what I call a healthy double shift. Hehehe!"

"Can't I finish what I was saying...doesn't anyone want to hear...did you see that program on the radio today?"

"He hasn't got much time left. I could tell right away. Just like Svanquist. Same yellow look. At the most one week, I said to the doctor. And he had to agree."

Somebody's leg can't be bent and points stiffly towards the fireplace. Somebody can't remember and thinks dinner is served at nine in the morning. Around midnight he waits in vain for his morning coffee.

"I walk to the gate and back every day. No matter what the weather's like. You've got to keep in shape!"

Why? The eyes all around ask. But no one dares say it out loud.

Like children, they go to bed before the late-evening news. The card players as well become restless at that time and start fishing for their gold watches in the tight little pockets of their vests. "To my dearest friend from his Ebba." "To our esteemed co-worker, the chief accountant of The Bank of Commerce..." And they jingle their one-crown stakes. "No, really, you guys, time flies, you know!"

A night of lonely pacing and sighing. Old men's melancholy odors rise into the darkness from their piles of clothes. The one who had repaired his underwear so artfully on the sewing machine is now a handful of ashes, her dead eyes look down from the wall. What's left of her silk pajamas is now a doily on his table.

Slowly, the morning light dries the tears of the night. Dream visions congeal to glue in the eyelashes. Breakfast trays are carried in and out by kind, nasty, patient, cheery, or pretentious girls. Somebody turns around and grunts. Somebody else has found his sleeping position forever.

"Miss, do you think I can get his bed? It's much better than mine."

Today that letter has to come. He imagines it already lying next to his lunch plate. The colorful airmail decorations will shine in his eyes today. Otherwise, it means that he no longer thinks about his old father. That's what he's told himself for a whole week already. No, a month. But he calls it a week, for the sake of the son. He can see the letter so clearly that some fine day he's going to open it and read it out loud for his table mates.

A big car draws some to the window. But it's only the doctor. A rumor lies on the breakfast trays like an invisible note. The night nurse is planning to quit.

"That bitch!"

"That wonderful woman!"

"She just about killed me with her constant enemas."

"Well, if it hadn't been for her, I wouldn't be alive today."

During the night somebody put his penis through his wedding ring. Not tolerating the pressure it had stiffened in surprise. Now he was squirming with pain and shame. "No, I'm not having any breakfast! Just go away. Go! Go!"

Two early birds wander arm in arm out on the steps. Slowly. That's the way. One step at a time.

"I'll never talk to Johnson again. Not after what happened last night..."

"Soon we can sit at the gate and feed the birds. Can you walk that far?"

The green curtains make the sickroom dark like an aquarium. Cautiously like a child, he caresses his friend's cheek.

"Get better now, Charlie. You'll be back on your feet soon. You'll see. We'll play a game of whist, you and I."

They babble and commiserate with their friend who is already halfway gone and barely manages to wander with his eyes in the room of the living. His fingers crease the top sheet into small tucks. They fumble around the monogram, but it isn't his. Fear fills the hollow at the back of his head with sweat. Yet his voice is firm when he says: "I am not afraid of death."

His unmarried daughter sits on a chair at his feet. Her thoughts are far away while she is trying to talk about such that could interest a half-dead father.

"Last night I went to the movies with a friend." (Beloved. Your hands. Soon, soon they will travel all over my body. Your smells made me forget the movie.)

"Father, did you hear what I said? Well, I said that I went to the movies. With a friend. No, not anyone you know."

Inaccessible, she is sailing inside the bubble of her happiness. The father is picking invisible flowers in the wrinkles of the sheet. He picks them and drops them again. Nothing left to see in his fingers. In his eyes a pale flame flutters.

"Please, nurse, tell me, my daughter, wasn't my daughter here just now?"

"She left an hour ago."

"Is that possible? No, nurse, not that... please not again..."

"Yes, Mr. Swensson, it's time for a shot. There, there, don't tense up so. It'll be over in a second. You'll hardly feel it at all. You've got to take your medicine when you're sick. And we do want to get better, don't we?"

"No-o-o. I don't want to. Please nurse, please don't."

The doors are thick. All is quiet in the corridor. Three fat bellies are parading there camouflaged in dress suits. One of them is holding a bouquet of carnations, mimosa, and freesia. There is a seventieth birthday party in room twenty-five.

"You'll soon be of age now, old man! Hahaha!"

"What the devil do you think you're doing here, Carlman? You're not invited, you know. No, really..."

A draft slams the door to the party. A faint smell of whiskey blends with the corridor atmosphere of floor wax and hygiene. Against a window the silhouette of a girl in white polishes brass handles.

The gardener removes the sacking from the rose bushes. A group of dignified ladies have come to have coffee with the superintendent.

"Dear child! How nice it is here!" The child blushes with resentment and spills his coffee on the saucer.

"They said that I wasn't invited. I've never been so insulted in my whole life."

He has managed to avoid much in his ninety years. Then, an experience like that had to wait for him behind the last bend.

"Okay, okay, don't get so excited. Just do like me. Go to classes. Get yourself educated. Makes you stay young. You've got to keep on doing something all the time. Get hold of something. Anything. Stamps. Golf. Art history. I've joined the bowling club. My son picks me up with the car once a week. We bowl over there, near the City Hall. I'm better than the fifty-year-olds. That's what they all say..."

Blabber pours from his mouth like dirty dishwater. He who was looking for comfort tries to shield himself even more desperately. Their battle of words continues until the iron clippers of the gate cuts it off.

The three congratulating stomachs are crowded on the same sofa and laugh with the same laugh. They look like gingersnaps that were too close on the cookie sheet and ran together. And, quite fittingly, they get up at the same time, and, together, bow out of the smoky party room.

In the elevator as well, they are forced to crowd together. They look like one single party-dressed lump behind the gilded bars of the elevator cage.

A little later they are standing in front of the north windows on the landing. Ruffled, they straighten their shoulders. Thoughtfully, they stroke their bellies, thirsty now for their whiskey glass. Anxiously, they look at the clock. Still fifty minutes to go before dinner. One of them picks his ear with a stretched-out little finger. Another brushes imaginary cake crumbs from his lapel.

"Stuffed cabbage?"

"What, again today?"

"Shall we go see Charlie?"

"Hell no. Take away our appetite."

The kindest of them winces in confusion and looks out the window. A flock of magpies are using the gardener's television antenna as a trapeze.

A son and his wife who could "just come on the run" zoom away making an elegant curve. The car shines blue like the wings of a mallard.

The sticky rose buds are freezing. How many will see them bloom?

"When I was young, I flew to America several times."

The spring green meets his statement with icy silence. The foliage is still sparse. You can see the fence through it in several places.

For one moment the world holds its breath. Then it turns away from the sun. It has had enough.

The Night Between the Second and the Third

I<small>T IS NOT UNCOMMON</small> to hear people talk about the exact day and moment of their conversion, or about the exact minute they fell in love. In this same way, I can point to a spot on the calendar—and on the map for that matter—where my life split into two separate parts, once and for all, and irrevocably. Before that, it had been quite stable, never simple, always vulnerable, but still, structurally, pretty much like other people's. After that date, the line of my life, were one to draw it, looked like a Y.

I had borrowed a house for the summer in a little fishing village, not far from the city of X. My friend, who was head of the municipal museum there, was taking part in an excavation near Civita Vecchia, and he had generously left his summer home at my disposal.

It was an old fisherman's cottage, built of stone and whitewashed. It had already, since the beginning of the century, been taken over by summer guests from

X, and had therefore lost some of the rustic simplicity which was the foremost quality of these coastal dwellings. The earthen and flagstone floors had been covered with linoleum. The large open fireplace, formerly used for baking, cooking and heating, had been replaced, first by a wood stove and then by an electric range, complete with modern kitchen fan and spice shelf made of teak.

Nevertheless, there was something about the very situation of the house, in the shade of two pitch-dark elms, protected by a boathouse with walls worn to a silver gray, and at a stone's throw from the others which were clustered along a very small village street, that made me feel as though transferred to another century. During the long sunny days I used to pretend I was Robinson Crusoe, just washed up on the beach, far from fellow human beings, news, and especially newspapers, which only served to remind me of my profession. I had unpacked only what was absolutely necessary, a pair of worn-out jeans and two sweaters. All of my more citified clothes remained unused. And I was barefoot, except for the few times when I took a car into X in order to replenish my supply of food and buy a few bottles of wine.

Now, to that spot on the calendar: the night between the second and the third of August 19—. Already, dark clumsy flocks of scoters were flying so close to the surface of the water that I mistook them for porpoises. The oyster-catchers on their fragile lacquer-red legs stepped carefully around in the debris left by the first autumn storm. The piles of seaweed gave off a strong odor of putrefaction, and fog seemed to stick in downy bits of fuzz to fences and elder trees for a long time after the sun had risen and dispersed it: it was the thousands of gossamers made visible by the dew.

Often it didn't get warm and clear until about eleven. Then the sun would shine butter-yellow in competition with the flat heads of the tansy that grew next to the cottage, and I spurned the green-stained bench in front of the cottage to sit instead on an old fish crate on the leeward side of the boathouse, with my morning coffee and my pipe, and look out over the southern part of the bay. Some mornings, the island of Bornholm lay there on the horizon, round and the size of a whale; other mornings, it had disappeared to visit unknown latitudes.

Towards evening on the second of August it started to blow and the breakers became more powerful, sputtering white foam against the deep blue August waters. At dusk the sea roared like constant thunder. On my radio I could hear storm warnings for the coast just south of X, and before I climbed into bed in an alcove up in the otherwise empty loft, I moved the window hook to the closest notch, so that the window was open by only a cautious crack.

Rocked by the rhythmical thudding of the waves, I fell asleep while reading *The Reminiscences of an Egoist*, and woke only for a minute to switch off the lamp and to turn over.

Out of this second and excellent sleep, which would be graded first class if subjected to a consumer evaluation regarding its stability, depth and durability, I was awakened at daybreak by a strange sound.

At night, the sounds in the village and on the adjoining heath, where my cottage was situated, were the following: the splashing, moaning or rushing of the sea, always rhythmical, like the heartbeats of an enormous mammal. Secondly, the crowing of the roosters, both those cocky 6 a.m. wake-up roosters belonging to my closest neighbor, a fisherman, and the bantam roosters that a summer family kept at the other end of the village. Thirdly, it happened that owls hooted, drowsy blackbirds called, cows mooed and early morning traffic swished by on its way to and from the main road in the distance.

Have I left out any sound or call? I'm trying to remember... Yes, the electric pump which took care of my water supply for shower, lavatory and kitchen sometimes decided to start groaning and coughing, even though no one had demanded its services.

I supported myself on my elbow and listened. The wind had increased, but I told myself that it would have to increase much more before the fishermen would refer to it as a storm. As though trying to free themselves from the leaves which constituted such a dangerous windbreak, the two elms twisted and shook their branches, and stretched and pulled at their roots. The window strained on its short leash. The surf broke with roaring force against the rocks on the beach with, it seemed to me, a constantly accelerating crescendo.

In between the worst of the roaring, in the lulls between the waves of sound, there were loud shouts.

Who would shout like that in the middle of the night? Nobody from the village. That was out of the question. Once at the beginning of summer a little summer-guest boy had got lost and screamed bloody murder. He had waked up and, finding himself alone, he had looked for his mother who was playing bridge in a house across the road. But that sort of noise was very unusual. The village was the quietest and most peaceful of places.

I lay down, closed my eyes and tried to ignore the image which inexorably developed even behind my closed lids: the image of a small sailing boat or other pleasure craft, adrift, out of control, about to be sucked out to sea by the dangerous current—or already pierced by the sharp-edged rocks furthest out on the point, and there, struggling, water up to his mouth, a father with a child in his arms, entangled in debris, and equally afraid of being sucked out again and of being hurled to death against the rocks.

There it was again. A shout strong and imploring. And now I did hear clearly that it was a cry for help, and not an inarticulate scream as I had first thought, but a completely clear "Help!"

He or she called whenever the sea was the slightest bit quieter, or else he called all the time, and it was only then, during the intervals, that I could hear that "Help!" which made the hair on my arms literally stand on end.

I didn't have the slightest idea about what to do. But I also realized that remaining inactive would be the same as committing murder. I am a landlubber and have neither the strength nor the equipment for any life-saving maneuver. Words like "lifelines," "life buoys," "storm lantern" crossed my mind. Where could I find these things? I had been thoroughly instructed about such problems as the care of the water pump, rubbish collection, forwarding the mail and defrosting the refrigerator. Heroic acts or tragedies had not been included in the plans for these holiday weeks. I wandered around now in the low-ceilinged loft, pulled on my jeans, cursed and searched for my sandals (which were outside under the garden bench), put on a sweater the wrong way and tried, in vain, to button it down the back with my arms at a grotesque angle, while now and then listening and hearing—not knowing whether what I feared most was hearing, or that the rhythmical, heart-rending call for "Help" had stopped.

"Help! Help!"

A catalogue of all the possible alternatives went through my head one more time, so reluctant was I to go out and wake the village people in order to fight the sea for the sake of the life of some foolhardy pleasure sailor. But the catastrophe throbbed like a pulse inside and outside my head, and I ran out into the black, roaring night and heard myself shouting just as heart-rendingly: "Help!"

A flickering silvery glow on the horizon meant that daybreak was on its way, but the heath, the village and the beach were still dark, and down by the cliffs you could only see the white bursts of the surf.

I must have seemed panic-stricken when, having finally succeeded in waking my neighbor the fisherman, a man in his sixties, I gasped and stammered what I wanted. I can still see the skeptical and thoughtful way he looked at me while sluggishly hitching up his pajamas so that I have to push him aside to get to the telephone, and it is only after having dialed the emergency number that I realize the telephone is right next to the ear of the curler-covered head of his sleeping wife.

She moans about something in a nightmare while I give my name, the name of the village, and tell them what I have heard.

First there is silence from the receiver, then a slow, dull voice says in dialect: "You seen them?"

"No," I scream. "Here, listen yourself!" And in stupid desperation I turn the receiver towards the door and then back to my face, and shout: "Don't you hear? They're screaming all the time!"

Of course there's silence from the receiver at that, but my neighbor takes it out of my hand and says with some authority: "I think it'd be a good idea if you came!"

Only then does the emergency man decide to do something, and says almost with alacrity: "O.K., we're coming."

In the meantime, my neighbor has put on his oilskins and picked up the lantern that apparently is always ready next to the front door, which has the week's TV program tacked to it, and as we struggle on our way against the wind, he says again and again: "Well, where are they?" But sometimes the storm makes words impossible, and he puts his hard warm hand on my ice-cold arm instead, and I point silently. "There. Way out there on the point."

I hear them still. "He-elp! He-elp! He-elp!" I hear that the voice is getting weaker and I run faster. But the point, which in calm and sunny weather is a favorite bathing area, is now under water, part of an underwater landscape made up of furrowed slabs of limestone leading to traps slippery as soap. I fall down, hurt myself and get wet through and through. I watch the lantern light up the waves and expect any second to see the wreck of a boat, or a panic-stricken white face, but there is nothing to see except leaden waves and white foam, and a silvery shimmer from the east which, getting stronger, makes the darkness less dense.

So they have drowned, after all.

The fisherman's wife must have awakened and alarmed the other neighbors. In the trembling light of dawn I can dimly see a little flock, and two unfamiliar men making their way through the people with poles and lifelines. I suppose they are the rescue men who've come by car. The sea is lit by our lanterns from one side and by the dawn from the other, there is no sign of a wreck, of debris from a boat, or of struggling human beings. And still, all the time, one can hear them, sometimes weaker, sometimes stronger, those wailing calls for help.

It could all have ended there, with the coming of the sun, the people on the beach, silent and irresolute, confronted with a mystery. But then my life would not have acquired the shape of a Y.

The fisherman's wife walks towards me and, in a manner quite devoid of irony or malice, rather kindly in fact, and a bit pityingly, says: "Wasn't it maybe the sheep you heard?"

At that, all of them turn towards land, and they start talking and laughing, and some of them curse ("Damn summer guests!"), so that I can hardly make out the rhythmical bleating from the farm up the road: Ba-a! Ba-a! He-elp! He-elp!

I don't know how I get back to my bed. I stumble away at a tremendous pace, and the talk and laughter fade, and I run up the steep staircase to the loft, throw myself headfirst onto the bed, and begin weeping like a child, with a misery from ages ago, a continuation of a crying fit from when I was twelve years old, when my teacher refused to believe me even though I tried to explain (that I had *not* tried to cheat when I had leaned over towards the boy next to me during a test, that I had only wanted to know what time it was...that I hadn't written "Mary stinks" even though it was I who was standing there, pen in hand, when he surprised us in the locker room). With a superhuman, self-hypnotic effort, I manage to sink back into that very sleep that I was enjoying before the shouting awakened me.

There I was again now, voluptuously stretched out on the wide mattress, under the low attic ceiling that smelled slightly of tar, completely embraced by sleep, rocked by the roaring of the sea, which apparently had decided to beat its own storm record, that night between the second and the third of August.

For a man alone on holiday in a house at a safe distance from the surf, that noise is merely a great rhythmical source of pleasure. "Just listen to the sea," I would mumble to a friend or lover, had one been with me. "Do you hear how beautifully it sings?"

But I was alone, sound asleep, and it was something entirely different from the roar of the surf that finally woke me. It was a shout.

I turned onto my side and supported my head with my hand. The window was open only a crack, but it was enough for me to hear a distinct shout. A human being was out there in the storm, screaming something. "He-elp! He-e-lp!"

I lay down again on my back and looked at the ceiling. It was pitch-dark, both outside and in the house. Nonsense, I thought. Nobody walks around here on the heath screaming for help! And if anyone was being shipwrecked, he certainly wouldn't be so naive as to think shouting like that would reach people's ears, what with all the noise from the sea.

But as I was lying there, almost falling asleep again, the shout returned, again and again, just as real as the pounding of the waves against the beach: "Help! Help!"

I got up and felt how the hair on my arms stood on end from fright and cold. Out there in those breakers, a human being was struggling for his life. Perhaps a whole family. A father who saw his little daughter being washed overboard, or who was already lying in the water with a baby in his arms, or maybe a dog...

I groped around for a warm sweater, managed to put both legs into one jeans leg and almost toppled like a tree being felled, bumped my forehead against the rough sloping ceiling, and all the time I heard those heart-rending shouts and saw in my imagination a man who was trying to swim as hard as he could with one arm, while the sea sucked him out and washed over him alternately, and he didn't know whether he wanted to reach or feared coming closer to the sharp rocks on the beach. From time to time, when he managed to fill his lungs with air, he uttered that piercing, wailing shout for help.

I opened the window wide, and it was immediately wrenched out of my hand, hitting the wall. A weak tinkling told me that the lower pane had been knocked out and fallen to the ground. As I leaned out to get hold of the window, I searched in vain in the darkness. Everything was black. Shouldn't a capsized boat have some sort of lantern, or a light at least? Stupid, I said to myself. The mast was most likely upside down already, caught between the two barnacle-covered rocks, five meters under the surface of the sea. In that case they can hold on to the keel, at any rate...but then, most likely, the keel is under water and as slippery as a soapy knife.

Anxious to find good reasons to just go back to bed and sleep, I finally tried to convince myself that the whole thing was a figment of my imagination. But I did keep hearing, again and again, those shouts for help. "Help!"

Who is a call like that for? For the one who hears it.

What other sounds could one hear in the village, if it wasn't... I went through them: the owl, the dogs, the roosters, the blackbirds (impossible), and while I continued my list I tightened my jeans belt as though in a trance, and thought about how inadequate I was, with my weak muscles, shortness of breath, to accomplish any sort of heroic action on a night like this, the night between the second and the third of August.

Didn't the shouts seem weaker now? And couldn't it mean that it was something else, or did it mean that the individual had got his mouth full of ice-cold sea water in the middle of his shout? Could I sit here, at the age of forty, in possession of all my senses, a Swedish man with Christian upbringing, and almost wish that the shouts would stop, so that I wouldn't have to do anything? Why, that was murder! In thought, at any rate.

Then I remembered the sheep. I was so relieved that I smiled into the darkness, there in my alcove. Of course! The sheep! A farmer up the road had acquired two sheep, a brown one and a gray one. They were of an unusual breed and were tethered next to the road, where they grazed on the lawn in front of the farmer's house. I'd heard their bleating for several days now.

Perhaps there wasn't any grass left, and it was time to move them.

How lucky that I remembered them! They were real. Not something I had imagined because of my laziness and cowardice in order to be spared going out into the stormy night! I laughed out loud at that—my having to reassure myself that they existed. Imagine if, before remembering the sheep, I had managed to wake my neighbor who was a fisherman, and his wife, or if I had phoned the rescue people who, on a stormy night like this, certainly had other things to think about than to rush out because of a false alarm!

Of course there was a 1-to-100 chance that what I had heard was human shouting, but the certainty was still 99 per cent in favor of the sheep, which towards daybreak usually stood there and called to each other: Ba-a! Ba-a-a! And it was typical of the newness of the situation that their bleating woke me. But then again, if there were a catastrophe, wouldn't I have been awakened by something so new as a catastrophe?

There they were again: Ba-a-a! He-e-elp! They alternated, first the sheep and then the human being in distress. But I had already taken off my jeans and was sitting on the edge of the bed with my head in my hands. For some reason I let my hands glide up to cover my ears, and so heard only the pounding of the surf, or was it my pulse?

Won't make a fool of myself, I was thinking. "Help!" came more weakly from those rocks where I had stood two days before with my fishing tackle and got two briskly fighting codfish. No. Not there. There was nothing but glitter and terns and scoters that swam over the tops of the waves in a black flock that made

THE NIGHT BETWEEN THE SECOND AND THE THIRD 147

me think of porpoises. How lucky that I remembered the sheep!

The next morning the storm had calmed down somewhat. I sat, as usual, on the leeward side of the boathouse on my old fish crate, leaning comfortably against the silver-gray planks worn velvet-soft by the weather. The coffee in my mug was steaming and my tape recorder on the rock surrounded by wild pinks was humming Bach's French suites. I thought I heard voices from the beach, so I got up to look around the corner of the boathouse—I can remember how the wind hit me in the face and made me think that it was still pretty strong—I saw almost the whole village population, and a car which in some incomprehensible way had managed to drive down there!

The sea was calmer and the wind had veered. Very distinctly I could see what it was all about. The mast of the sailing boat was leaning at a 45-degree angle from the outermost point of the rock. Where I had stood with my fishing tackle, two strangers, apparently those who had come in the car, were trying to tie someone to a stretcher. I both wanted and didn't want to see what had happened. All at once I remembered everything: the shouts and my cowardice. The sheep! Oh, I...

I kept to myself all day. But it was no use. Exactly at sundown, my neighbor the fisherman came over, bursting with the terrible happenings in the sea just outside his house and mine.

I had to make coffee and we spiked it with a shot of whiskey. We drank and looked thoughtfully past each other, he at the wall behind me, and I out through the window towards the rocks where the mast had fastened like the hand of a broken clock. And all the time I felt as though it was stuck like a needle through my throbbing heart.

"And nobody heard anything," he sighed, saying goodbye. And again, "Just think, nobody heard anything!"

I didn't answer. You usually don't have to. Those who want to talk usually do both: ask the questions and answer them too.

"It's that there's so much. The sea roars and the old lady snores. There's so much noise. And one's so tired one sleeps so soundly. Well, well. And all that time, those poor people..."

And so at the end, like a persistent coda to a sonata, when we were already standing in the doorway, and I was almost pushing him out in the direction of his house and the village: "And I didn't hear anything. No. Not a damned thing."

And then he turns around in the middle of the burnt August grass, stands like a black and threatening silhouette in the light of the setting sun, and looking straight at me, although I can't see his face, he fires his last shot: "And you, how come you didn't hear anything?"

There is a long pause, and it is then that I understand that my life has acquired the shape of a Y. And I will never know which of the Y's two branches I live in. I didn't then and I won't in the future.

This happened during the night between the second and the third of August a few years ago. I have had lots of time to think about my Y-shaped destiny, and it seems clear that my life, like the wick of a candle, was twined of two separate pieces of yarn from the beginning. One of them stands for indifference, and the other for feeling and concern. It was only after the happenings between the second and the third that the two separated, and they are now free from each other, in eternal opposition.

From that night on, sheep have always been human beings for me, and human beings sheep, if you understand what I mean. Shouts for help will always sound like bleating, and the peaceful sounds sheep make will sound like screams of tragedy. Whichever way I turn, I've been unable since then either to look the other way or to give a helping hand, and my Christian conscience is on a constant electric trampoline, just like those mice we've all read about, who are made to jump up on the charged bar in order to get to their food; sometimes they get a shock, at other times only their food.

Whatever I do, however I jump, I get a shock, a slap in the face, and I try in vain to keep my balance.

A NOTE ABOUT THE AUTHOR

The winner of many literary awards in Sweden, Margareta Ekström is a novelist, short story writer, diarist, and poet, as well as a literary critic and columnist. She has published nine volumes of short fiction in Swedish. English translations of some of her stories have appeared in *London Magazine, Vogue,* and *The Ontario Review.* She lives in Stockholm with her husband, the editor and writer Per Wästberg, and their two children.